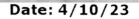

KIELI

The Dead Sleep in the Wilderness

Yukako Kabei

created by: Shunsuke Taue

CHAPTER 1:
ROOMMATE

"So we'll test him to see if he'll die or not."
"What if he's a normal human?"
"If he dies, we'll know he was normal."

CHAPTER 2:
MAY I SEE YOUR TICKET?

"Why didn't you show him your ticket?"
"Show who?"
"'Who'...?"

CHAPTER 3:
CHEERS FOR
THE BLOOD-
COVERED
CLOWN

"Have any clowns ever
died in this town?"

CHAPTER 4:
"I'M HOME."

Not sleeping meant that the world never pauses; there's no sense that today will end or tomorrow will come. She wondered what it would feel like to live in that monotonous time flow for decades.

CHAPTER 5:
THE DEAD SLEEP
IN THE WILDERNESS

But there was light from outside there — it was a dim light, hidden in sand-colored clouds, but the color of the earth and sky that had cherished the planet's scarcely remaining resources, storing them in their bosom, poured down in a sparkling ray. And anyway, he had the vague idea that if he could get under that light, everything would be okay.

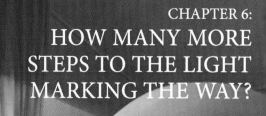

God is a man of such perfect, flawless character that he only watches over everyone equally — the strong and the weak, the rich and the poor — and never plays favorites or reaches His hand out to any of them.

Oh, what a wonderful God. He can just drop dead.

KIELI

The Dead Sleep in the Wilderness

YEN ON

NEW YORK

KIELI: The Dead Sleep in the Wilderness
YUKAKO KABEI

Translation: Alethea Nibley and Athena Nibley

KIELI Vol. 1
© YUKAKO KABEI / KADOKAWA CORPORATION ASCII MEDIA WORKS 2003
Edited by ASCII MEDIA WORKS
First published in Japan in 2003 by
KADOKAWA CORPORATION, Tokyo.
English translation rights arranged with
KADOKAWA CORPORATION, Tokyo,
through Tuttle-Mori Agency, Inc., Tokyo.

English translation © 2009 by Yen Press, LLC

Yen On
1290 Avenue of the Americas
New York, NY 10104
www.YenPress.com

Yen On is an imprint of Yen Press, LLC.
The Yen On name and logo are trademarks of
Yen Press, LLC.

First Yen On Edition: July 2009

ISBN: 978-0-7595-2929-8

10 9 8 7 6 5 4

OPM

Printed in the United States of America

WHY ISN'T GOD HERE?

On this planet, there is a Church, but no God. Kieli realized this fact when she was four or five years old, and she always thought it strange for a world to have such a prominent church even when it seemed so obvious there was no God. When she was seven, she finally hit on a very satisfactory answer to her dilemma.

"Grandmother, after I heard the sermon today, I finally figured it out." In her excitement, Kieli would sometimes skip or twirl around as she announced her brilliant discoveries to her grandmother on their way home from church.

That day, the head priest had given a sermon on the Church's history. Apparently, a spaceship carrying the legendary "Eleven Saints and Five Families" had landed on this godless planet hundreds of years ago and built a church. But that ship had left its mother planet hundreds of years before that, and the very patient Saints had traversed the universe for many generations before arriving. Now no one remembered the name of that place.

"God wasn't very patient, was He? I think our planet was so far away, He got tired and went home before He got here. I wonder why the important people in the Church can't figure it out. It's so simple! Do they think that God will stay with them forever?"

"Kieli," her grandmother said quietly, walking beside her. She would repeat her granddaughter's name like this whenever she did something she wasn't supposed to. She would never yell or lecture. Without changing her expression or her gaze, she would just say, "Kieli," in a sad, quiet voice.

Kieli had promised that she would never, ever talk about the absence of God when she was outside of the house. If she talked like that, she had been told, "the Church's Soldiers would gouge her heart out." The warning that this is what happened to bad children who didn't keep God's teachings was a story adults used to make their children behave. It came from the legend of the Undying, demon soldiers who killed many people in the War long, long ago, and had been defeated only when their hearts had been torn out.

"I'm sorry, Grandmother. I won't say it anymore." Dejected, Kieli shut her mouth, stopped skipping, and faced forward. But what Kieli was sorry about was that she had gotten carried away and broken her promise; that childish threat never scared her a bit.

There was a reserved kind of bustle on the streets as worshippers walked home on Sunday morning. They all wore hats of myriad shapes to worship in and bundled themselves up in dark-colored overcoats. The Colonization Days holiday was approaching once again, and the air was beginning to carry the scent of winter. To Kieli, the smell of winter was the smell of the smog spewed out by fossil fuels. An exhaust pipe stuck out of the roof of every building that lined either side of the street and sent thick gray smoke into the sky.

Kieli turned around again and walked backward for a little while. Pushing back the brim of her hat and looking up, she could see the grand and imposing domed roof of the cathedral standing in the center of the town, peeking out between the other buildings.

Suddenly, behind her there rose a commotion. The jeers and screams in the distance drew closer, and as she turned around in surprise to see what was going on, a man pushed aside a passerby that had been walking ahead of Kieli and jumped out right in front of her.

"Wah!"

Kieli instinctively drew herself back, and then . . .

Fwa-boom!

If she'd been forced to describe the sound of such an explosion, she'd have said it was like the heavy atmosphere being tightly compressed and released all at once. The sound roared through the morning street.

Before her eyes, Kieli saw the man's chest burst open. Through the gaping, round hole, she could see men covered from head to toe in strange white armor. Wisps of smoke rose from the barrels of several guns aimed her way. She heard a woman gasp somewhere, but Kieli just stood there, unable to remember to breathe, let alone scream. Finally, she managed to stagger backward and fall back onto the paved street. As if in response, the man fell to his knees, then collapsed at Kieli's feet. His neck was bent at an unnatural angle, and his face turned toward her. His unfocused gaze rested on the air in front of Kieli.

As someone came running toward her, Kieli regained her senses and the crowd's stirring came back to her, as if she'd just remembered how to hear after a temporary loss.

"Kieli, are you hurt?" her grandmother asked as she knelt beside Kieli and embraced her. Her aged, wizened hands trembled slightly. Kieli took her hand and answered in a monotone that she was fine.

Amidst intermingling whispers of both fear and awe, the crowd moved aside, and metallic footsteps echoed as the armored men marched through their center. Kieli, still sitting, watched them, and as a corner of her mind thought, "Oh, they're coming this way," she returned her gaze to the fallen man.

Something had rolled out from the hole in the man's chest.

It was a black stone, about the size of an adult fist. It wasn't unlike a strange machine component. A few torn, narrow tubes that looked like both cables and blood vessels hung from it, and a thick liquid that resembled used oil puddled around it. Inside the stone, a dull, amber-colored light blinked rhythmically, like a heartbeat.

She unconsciously reached out for it, but another hand

snatched it up first. It was a grim, armored hand, wearing a white gauntlet made of special metal fiber. When she looked up, a soldier was mumbling something inside his mask. *We have just executed a wicked man. There is nothing to worry about. You didn't see anything.* She thought they said something like that, but none of it stayed in Kieli's mind.

After that, no matter what she did, she couldn't remember the face of the man who had died right in front of her. Only the mysterious black stone and his open, empty eyes remained, burned forever onto her memory.

CHAPTER 1

ROOMMATE

Miss Hanni was a teacher, almost thirty years old, who wore her hair tied back in a bun and angular, rimless glasses. Aside from her tendency to be melodramatic and her love of pop quizzes, she was a virtuous and devout believer. But to Kieli, "devout believer" was not a compliment.

"My goodness, Kieli! Honestly, whatever is the matter with you?"

Honestly, whatever is the matter with you? My Lord. Oh, what are we to do with you? For a while now, Miss Hanni had been lamenting the state of affairs with repetitions from her limited collection of phrases, looking up at the ceiling with exaggerated gestures, and taking off her glasses to dab at her eyes with her handkerchief.

"Not only are you late, but dressed the way you are. Don't tell me you didn't know about today's service."

"I'm sorry, Miss Hanni," Kieli apologized, checking her desire to say, "I didn't know." She wanted to avoid giving lame excuses and having a pointless argument with her teacher. After all, it would look bad to say it was because no one had told her (even if that was the truth).

A few of her classmates snickered in the three rows behind Miss Hanni. They all wore their beautifully embroidered, white choir uniforms; Kieli alone was dressed in the normal black bolero with its big collar. The plain, black uniform had its own kind of dignity when everyone was wearing it, but right now, Kieli looked like a witch-in-training, wearing a cheap robe, who'd been thrown into a chorus of angels.

The parish's head priest would be giving a congratulatory address on the first day of the Colonization Days holiday, so the service was not being held at the school's auditorium but rather in the cathedral in the center of town. Kieli and the other ninth-graders at the boarding school would be singing the hymns, so they were to wear their white choir uniforms and meet in time for rehearsal. The announcement was made at the student assembly last week, but Kieli was in detention doing a report and thus absent. The school dorms were double rooms, so normally it wouldn't have been a problem for one of the roommates to miss an assembly. Unfortunately, Kieli didn't have a roommate, and neither her classmates nor her neighbors were kind enough to tell her. She was used to it, and she didn't feel like crying to her teacher over every little incident.

"Well, there's nothing we can do about it now. As long as you're sorry, we'll let it go this time. Don't let it happen again." Maybe she'd made the right choice in opting not to make excuses, because Miss Hanni left it at that and let Kieli off the hook surprisingly easily.

"Now don't dawdle. Get in line. The service is starting. Go to the back where you'll stand out as little as possible."

"Yes, ma'am." Kieli gave a quick bow as she passed by her teacher and took her place in the very back row of the choir. To her right, the freckle-faced, frizzy-haired Zilla let out a short laugh through her upturned nose. No doubt she was one of the girls who'd laughed earlier.

Blond-haired Becca suddenly appeared at her left. She glanced at Kieli, raised the skirt of her own black uniform, and winked as if to say, "It happened to me, too."

Kieli blinked at her for a second, then looked at Becca and let out a small, wry grin. It wasn't as if Becca wearing the black uniform would help Kieli at all, but it cheered her up a little. Sensing Zilla's dubious glare from her right, she suppressed her smile, erased the expression from her face, and turned forward.

The choir stood on raised platforms against the wall, so even from the back row, she could look out over the inside of the majestic central cathedral. A high, arched ceiling capped the white concrete walls. She'd heard that the impressive stained glass covering the walls to the right and left and the electric lights designed to look like candles were gifts from the Church in the capital. In the front, the black-robed priests were in neat lines on both sides of the pulpit, and behind them, the general congregation packed tightly into the pews. The diversely shaped hats of the parishioners wove together in an artless, uneven wave in contrast to the uniformity of the priests.

It baffled Kieli as much as ever that so many people would gather in reverence of a mother planet whose name they couldn't even remember and a God whose name they'd long since forgotten, but she didn't speak thoughtlessly of those things the way she used to. As far as Kieli knew, she was the only person who'd realized that there was no God in this church, and the Church's prestige continued, unwavering, to this day.

The rustling noise of the worshippers' whispers that had filled the space suddenly fell silent. The white-robed head priest appeared from behind a curtain and proceeded to the pulpit at a leisurely pace.

Kieli hid her grimace at the reverent sighs that escaped the silent congregation here and there. She'd seen the head priest many times since she was small, but she couldn't reconcile what was so holy about him that would elicit such appreciation of him from people. He was an aging man with thinning hair, and his stout build gave him a kind of dignity. Anyone passing him on the street, though, probably wouldn't think of him as anything more than a man getting on in years with a decent amount of wealth.

For one thing, if he had any kind of sacred, divine insight, how could he fail to notice *that*? There was no better evidence that the Church possessed no holy powers than *that*, weaving in and out of the chapel during prayers as if it owned the place.

Shifting her gaze, Kieli could see the image of a man with a rope around his neck, floating in the air above the head priest's head. Swollen blood vessels colored his face a dark red as he peered with great interest at the manuscript from which the head priest was reading.

The hanged ghost lifted his face as if he'd felt her gaze. His eyes met Kieli's, and his red, blood-swollen lips twisted in a crescent-shaped grin.

Kieli glared expressionlessly back at the hanged ghost and refocused her attention on the head priest. Even his oh-so-wonderful sermon that spoke so grandly of death and rebirth didn't leave any deep impressions; it just sounded phony to her ears.

Kieli.

She heard a voice calling her name.

Kieli, it's starting.

"Eh?"

When she came to herself, Kieli looked in the direction of the voice and saw Becca's blue eyes, like the glass eyes of a doll, winking at her from the end of the choir row. At the edge of her field of vision, Miss Hanni's rimless glasses glared angrily at her as if to say, "Am I still going to have to talk to you before you're satisfied?"

The next thing she knew, the organ's accompaniment had started and the choir began singing "The Song of Our First Blessings." Kieli panicked and started dragging the lyrics from her memory, practically lip-synching along with the alto chorus, and looked over at Becca standing next to her.

Becca stood as straight as she could, looking directly ahead, and her beautiful voice happily sang the soprano part. Kieli's row wasn't singing the soprano part, and Becca's lyrics were a little off, but no one but Kieli would pay it any mind.

After the service ended, it would be the Colonization Days holiday that her whole class looked forward to so much.

To Kieli, it would be just another boring, melancholy ten days.

At any rate, Becca was in a good mood today. Apparently she was going to see the sights in Westerbury during the holidays. Her parents and younger brother had gone on ahead and were waiting for her to meet up with them.

At the moment she was rambling on about Westerbury being a city that had developed cable networking and audio-visual technology, and how when the sun went down, screens on building walls projected sparkling colors that shifted dizzyingly along the streets as far as the eye could see. Something about a wondrous ice cream inlaid with pieces of stars being all the rage. Something about some experiential theater that just opened and how she was going to see a show there with her family at the end of her stay.

Kieli mostly ignored Becca as she bragged about her sightseeing plans, interjecting the occasional "Hmm" or "Wow." She couldn't imagine what someone would experience at an experiential theater or how it would be experienced, so Kieli had no idea if it was really worth all the excitement. The ice cream trend was the one thing that held some slight interest for her, but Becca veered away from that subject the second she brought it up.

"You can expect a souvenir, Kieli."

While Kieli was using all the imagination she had to picture what ice cream inlaid with pieces of stars would look like, Becca stopped boasting for a minute and turned to face her, her coat twirling as she moved.

"What would you like?"

"I don't need anything," Kieli refused vaguely.

Becca pouted. "Aww, you could ask for something." Her sleeves fluttered in the wind as she turned and resumed her jaunty walk down the street.

Becca was a pretty girl. Today, instead of the school-designated travel clothes, she wore a brilliant red coat and carried, as expected, not the school-designated bag, but a brown Boston bag. As for Kieli, over her usual uniform she wore the school-designated black duffle coat, and the unfriendly bag (which most students preferred not to use because of its resemblance to a mail sack) hung diagonally across her shoulder. Becca's supple, blond hair fell in waves down to her waist and looked stunning against her red coat. Kieli's hair was long and black and just hung artlessly down her back. Becca was tall and attractive. On the other hand, if her class were to line up according to height, Kieli would be a little ahead of the center.

If someone on the street were to catch sight of Becca and Kieli walking together, there is no doubt they would think Kieli was exceedingly plain next to the girl as lovely as a fashion doll.

But apparently Kieli was the only one thinking of such trivial things. The passersby paid no special attention to the two girls and quickly walked on by, turning up the collars of their coats.

It was the first afternoon of the Colonization Days holiday, and people hunched over as they walked along the streets of Easterbury, all bundled up for winter. Still, there was a sense of merriment in the air. Those who could take long holidays would be traveling with their families, and those who couldn't most likely planned to go home early to spend a leisurely evening indoors.

The Colonization Days came every year as the seasons readied themselves to step through winter's door.

The planet had greeted hundreds of winters since the Saints' ship made its autumnal landing. The story was that, thanks to the abundant fuel resources they mined from the planet's strata, the planet used to be highly advanced. But before long, a war broke out over those resources, and the long war itself ate up almost all of them. That happened long before Kieli was born.

All anyone could mine on the planet now were the dregs of inefficient fossil fuels. Bundles of exhaust pipes projected from the roofs of all the houses, coughing up thick, yellowish-gray smoke as if to paint a sky already the same color.

The train station's clock tower came into view at the end of the main street, sandwiched between buildings to the right and left. People holding large bags were sucked under the vaulted roof; they were most likely going to spend the holidays in a different town. The station building had been remodeled just a few years ago when it adopted a new railroad line, and a magnificent domed roof matching the design of the central cathedral rose toward the sky. To Kieli, it was needlessly magnificent, and she felt she would still be more comfortable with the old abandoned station building on the other side of town with its simple and unfriendly concrete walls.

She went around the rotary, casually gazing at the three-wheeled taxis (these, too, used fossil fuels with frighteningly bad gas mileage and carried cylindrical fuel tanks resembling unexploded bombs on their roofs) waiting for wealthy passengers in front of the station. When the entrance to the station drew near, a man's silhouette unexpectedly caught her attention. He was sitting on a bench toward the front, his head hanging down.

Kieli stopped walking for a second.

"Is something wrong? I'm leaving, you know." Becca looked curiously back at her from a few steps ahead.

"Yeah . . . He's dead. . . ." Kieli murmured shortly before she began walking again.

At this time of year, if anyone bothered to look, they could find the frozen corpse of at least one homeless wanderer somewhere in town every morning. They were generally elderly people, but the dead body on the bench still looked fairly young. He might be a seminary student. Seminarians from the university in the capital came on study pilgrimages for their priesthood exams, after all.

But then, a seminarian on a study pilgrimage would never die in the street, and considering his casual attire consisting of a nylon half-coat and rough workpants, along with his rusty, copper-colored hair, she couldn't really say he was a proper seminarian. Regardless, the girls at her boarding school recognized all men about his age as seminarians, so, for lack of any better ideas, Kieli decided to think of him as a seminary student.

The seminary student had expired where he sat, his back leaning heavily into the bench and his head drooping. He must not have had any unfinished business, because she couldn't see his spirit around anywhere. Kieli had mixed feelings when she caught herself confirming that so casually. Most people wouldn't see a dead body and start looking for its ghost.

"Ugh, Kieli!" Becca urged.

Kieli picked up her pace and passed in front of the bench. She would inform a station attendant later. Then they would contact the priests in charge of body disposal who would come clean it up.

Kieli was only a few steps past the bench when she stopped again. Out of the corner of her eye, she felt like she saw the

corpse move. She thought it was her imagination. *I mean, there's no doubt about it. He's dead.*

She turned her head back stiffly and stared at the body on the bench.

To Kieli's surprise, the seminary student on the bench slowly raised his eyelids. He twisted his neck as he took in his surroundings, a groggy look on his face. Finally, he stood and turned toward a now very rigid Kieli.

Eyes the same copper color as his hair met hers.

"Eek!"

Kieli let out an involuntary twitch of a scream. A second later, she started shrieking that a corpse had come to life in a voice that rang throughout the entire rotary in front of the station. The seminarian slipped off the bench, then, recovering from his daze, rushed to cover Kieli's mouth.

"I'm really very sorry, sir. She's just a little weird."

Becca had no right to call her weird. Forced to stand next to Becca as she smoothed things over, acting as if she was the mature one, Kieli stared sullenly at the tips of her shoes. When Becca admonished, "Come on, Kieli, say you're sorry," she had no choice but to bow her head and say, "I'm very sorry." Her head still down, she turned up her eyes to glance at the seminary student.

Thrusting one hand in his coat pocket and ruffling his hair with the other, the seminary student spit out, "Well, it's fine now," with a sigh. After being roused abruptly by the screaming girl in front of the station, he'd been accosted by the station attendants who came running to her aid, treated him like a suspected criminal, and nearly arrested him. So, having suffered enough calamities for the day, his face still bore quite a scowl for somebody saying, "It's fine."

Becca had introduced herself as Rebecca, the full name she used only when she had some ulterior motive, and had introduced Kieli as her roommate, almost as an afterthought. In exchange, they learned that the seminarian was named Harvey.

Seminarians were candidates to be leaders in the capital, and to the girls at the boarding school, getting to know one was kind of a status symbol. A group of trainees once came from the university at the capital to participate in a worship service in Easterbury, and Kieli's classmates ignored the service to whisper things like, "That tall one, second from the right! He's gorgeous!" They even had a popularity vote. It goes without saying that they had to endure a lengthy lecture from Miss Hanni that afternoon in homeroom and that the whole class had to write essays reflecting on what they'd done. (Kieli, who hadn't participated in the uproar, suffered with all the rest.)

So of course Becca was in high spirits over this fortunate encounter and one-sidedly lamented in exaggerated tones the fact that she had to leave Easterbury.

"Will you be in Easterbury until the Colonization Days are over? It would be nice if we could talk again after I get back."

"Oh, I'm leaving tomorrow. Going the opposite direction of Westerbury," the seminarian said without the slightest hesitation, easily crushing Becca's hopes. As other people bustled across the platform, Becca stood stock-still. "I see." She hung her head in disappointment, and her actions reeked of those of the heroine of a romance novel who'd resolved to leave her lover behind to go to the city. Kieli got a bit uncomfortable standing there and let her eyes wander.

As travelers heading toward Westerbury pushed their large bags onto the passenger car and boarded the train, they looked annoyed at Kieli, who blocked their way in front of the car as she talked to her companions. Busily making the rumbling, exhaust-spouting noises of fossil-fuel power, the train announced its departure.

"Will you be boarding?" a railroad worker in a conductor's uniform asked in a somewhat irritated tone, leaning half his body out of the last car.

The seminary student answered with a "No," adding a "Take care," and the conductor turned next to Kieli. "And you, miss? Will you be boarding?" When Kieli shook her head, the conductor nodded and rang the bell to announce their departure.

"Hey! Wait, wait! I'm boarding," Becca cried in dismay. She lifted her Boston bag in both hands and hurried onto the passenger car steps. As the departure bell rang across the platform sounding much like an alarm clock, she turned reluctantly back to bid farewell to Kieli and the seminarian. "See you, Kieli. You'll be okay without me, right?"

Kieli's answer of "I'll be fine" was drowned out by the sound of the bell and the tumult on the platform. It didn't even reach her own ears, so instead of repeating herself, Kieli simply nodded. Becca nodded back in understanding and turned next to face the seminary student. "Harvey, I pray we'll meet again."

The seminarian said a few words in response, but Kieli couldn't catch them. Apparently Becca did hear them, however. Kieli didn't know what he'd said to her, but her beautiful face lost its expression abruptly as she looked down at them from the train.

The bell suddenly stopped ringing. A strange moment of silence reigned over the platform, and then the train slowly started to slide away.

Even after the train started moving, Becca remained there, floating in the place where she had first gone up the steps. The walls of the cars that ran by passed smoothly through Becca's body one after another, like an illusion.

To be more accurate, it was Becca's body that was like an illusion.

Her best red coat and her Boston bag, her plans to meet with her parents and brother, the new theater, the ice cream, the souvenir she was thinking of getting for Kieli — everything about Becca's travel plans was nothing more than a game of pretend that she'd made up for her own amusement. Becca's body for wearing coats and her hands for carrying luggage were actually already at the bottom of her grave, and Becca had forever lost the ability to spend holidays with her family and stuff her cheeks with ice cream.

From his post in the last car, the conductor stared dubiously at Kieli and the seminary student standing there until, finally, he too passed through Becca's body.

"You're stupid," Becca said, her expression still blank. "I just wanted to pretend I was going on a trip. It's not like you're really a seminarian, either, stupid!" The abusive words she spat from her comely lips could only be considered a parting insult, and Becca floated down from where the train had been, then suddenly ran toward them. Kieli drew back automatically, but right before Becca crashed into her nose, her image vanished, and her formless presence blew through the ticket barrier with a gust of air.

All that was left on the platform were Kieli, the seminarian, the moderate chatter of those who'd seen people off, and their footsteps as they headed home.

"I never once said I was a seminarian. . . ." the man muttered to himself in annoyance. Then he noticed Kieli gazing at him as she stood beside him and glanced sideways at her.

Kieli looked up at her tall companion and asked, "What did you say to Becca?"

"All I did was ask how long I had to play along with this travesty," the man answered with an exasperated sigh, picking up his own luggage — an unusually small backpack for a traveler and, for some reason, a small, old radio.

"I don't like to meddle in other people's affairs too much, but . . . it's better not to bother with spirits like that; just ignore them. If you don't, they get carried away and never leave you alone."

"You should have told me that before this spring."

At Kieli's response, the man sneered, "Don't talk nonsense," and started walking away, joining the thin stream of people leaving the station. Kieli trotted after him, her shoulder bag bouncing against her lower back.

"You're not surprised about Becca?"

"To my mind, you're more of a surprise. You have a strong spiritual sense?"

Kieli nodded. "But my grandmother told me not to let too many people know. She's dead now, though."

"Yeah. It's less trouble that way."

"Hey, can you see other dead people? How do you know so much?" She naturally became more talkative than usual as she tried to keep up with the man's athletic pace. This was the first time she'd met anyone other than herself who could see that world, and based on what her grandmother said, there weren't that many of them, so she felt something of a kinship with this Harvey person.

Harvey, on the other hand, must've felt differently because he stopped momentarily and let out a sigh of very obvious annoyance. ". . . Hey. Well, I can't say I don't know how you feel, but I'm sorry. I have no intention of getting mixed up with a spirit-sensitive little girl. Now go home, do your sixth-grade homework, and have a nice holiday. Good-bye," he declared without a shred of the sincerity expected of one who "knew how she felt." Kieli had stopped in spite of herself; he left her there and resumed his long stride. Without looking back once, he disappeared through the station's gaping, square exit into the white outside.

"Ah . . ." This brought her high spirits to a surprisingly sudden and crashing demise, and she stood there, alone under the station's domed ceiling.

After standing in a daze for a while, she slowly began seething with anger. *He didn't have to say it like that. He really is nothing like a seminary student. Seminary students are friendlier and more gentlemanly.*

And who is he calling a sixth-grader? I know I have the build of a sixth-grader, but still. Kieli'd heard rumors that after they measured her height last spring, Miss Hanni doubted whether or not she was really fourteen years old and checked her citizenship form. If that was true, it would be extremely rude, and even if it wasn't true, it would be rude for a rumor like that to be going around as if it was.

Kieli gradually lost track of what she was angry about, and, feeling downhearted, she set off toward home.

Becca didn't come back (she was often quick to take offense and disappear, but she would usually be grinning close behind Kieli again in no time) as Kieli walked back to the boarding school alone. Kieli realized that she hadn't walked around town completely alone like this since Becca's spirit started haunting her last spring. In the corner of her mind, she thought about how unexpectedly lonely and boring it was not to hear Becca's voice chattering away next to her.

Kieli hadn't had any pleasant memories of the Colonization Days holidays since her grandmother's death six years ago, but this year had gotten off to the worst possible start, as if foreshadowing an even more awful holiday than former years.

She had Miss Hanni lecturing her first thing in the morning, she had the uncomfortable experience of wearing a different uniform than everyone else, Becca was still in a bad mood and wouldn't show herself, and to top it all off, sitting across from her at dinner was freckle-faced Zilla and her little minion of a roommate, the two girls Kieli hated most of all the girls at the boarding school (there was no doubt the feeling was mutual). Normally, she was careful to sit away from them, but during the long holiday, ninety percent of the students went back home to their families, and the remaining ten percent gathered at one table in a corner of the empty cafeteria, whispering to each other as they ate dinner.

The students that didn't go home to their families were generally students with no families to go home to. They were children with no relatives, who were allowed to attend the boarding school with financial assistance from the Church. And as far as Kieli knew, children with no relatives were generally the rebellious type. Instead of rallying together with others under similar circumstances, they would rather drag someone down by the ankles just so they could say that they were at least better off than *that* girl.

That being the case, no matter how hard anyone tried, there was no way a gathering of students like that would enjoy a meal in peaceful harmony, and after managing to endure the tense atmosphere of mealtime, Kieli escaped the cafeteria. The other students were still sluggishly cleaning up their trays as they insulted the students who weren't there.

She quickly returned to her room, and when she opened the door, Becca was lounging on the top of the bunk beds that occupied half of the small dormitory.

"Welcome back!" she said in her usual cheerful voice, as if nothing had happened that afternoon.

Kieli, after standing and gaping in the doorway for a second, complained insincerely, ". . . Aww, here it was so nice and quiet," and closed the door. She hated to admit it, but she had been a little worried about Becca after she vanished at the station, and for some reason she felt a bit disappointed.

Becca floated through the top bunk's mattress and sat on the bottom bunk. The bottom bunk was Kieli's bed, and Kieli, who wasn't especially messy or especially neat, had made the bed, arranging its modest bedding with about seventy percent thoroughness (when she had extra time, she could do ninety percent; when she slept in, about fifty).

The top bunk was empty, and a thin layer of dust lay on its yellowed mattress.

When she advanced to ninth grade and this room had been assigned to her, her roommate hadn't even lasted a week before crying to the teachers and begging for a different one. Her reason was that she could hear a strange girl's voice in the middle of the night. But no matter how thoroughly the teachers investigated, they couldn't hear any suspicious voices. Unable to get them to listen, the roommate ended up transferring to a school in a different town.

Since then, to an outsider it would seem that Kieli had become the only student in the boarding school with the luxury of having a double room all to herself. Kieli learned a little later that a female student two years her senior had died in a train accident the year before last, and there was no one on the top bunk of the room for a year until she and her roommate moved in. That's when Kieli finally understood who the beautiful blond girl was who looked so becoming in the black school uniform — this girl who was already staying in the room, doing something like living in it and acting as if she owned it, when Kieli got there.

And of course it was Becca who scared away Kieli's roommate, who had obtained the top bunk through a game of rock-paper-scissors, all for the truly simple (and if you asked her, legitimate) reason that the bed was hers. After that, she was so happy that Kieli could see her that she went ahead and treated her like a roommate, and followed her to class, to worship services, and on outings.

Kieli's lack of a roommate to give her messages from the assemblies, and the reason her classmates avoided the creepy girl who had no problem living in a room with ghost voices — thinking about it, it was all because of Becca's self-centered personality. If someone were to ask if Kieli had lots of friends until eighth grade, the answer would be a resounding no, but in ninth grade Kieli became a true lone wolf. Though, ironically, thanks to the presence of Becca (the cause of it all) Kieli didn't feel all that lonely.

"What happened after I left, Kieli? Did you talk about anything with that rude jerk?" Becca asked, rolling onto her side, resting her head in her hands over Kieli's pillow and acting sulky. Of course it was just a pose, and there were no actual indents on the pillow.

"Not really. He went off somewhere," Kieli answered vaguely, pulling out the chair at her study desk and sitting on it. It was just a steel chair, difficult to describe as suited for studying, but she maintained some comfort from it by fastening a worn-out cushion to the seat.

The traveler, "Harvey," or whatever his name was, who was so rude to Becca, had also been pretty rude to Kieli, so she didn't want to think about him anymore. He said he was going in the opposite direction of Westerbury tomorrow, so he would probably be getting on a train heading east that afternoon. *Just get lost already.*

"Seriously, it was just a little game. Why couldn't he have played along? And he couldn't have been too upset about getting a taste of what it's like to be pampered like a seminarian."

Becca continued to complain huffily from the bed, but Kieli wouldn't talk about it anymore. She turned to her desk and pulled her Church history notebook out of a drawer. She looked at the printout pressed between the pages and sighed.

Talking about that man reminded her she had homework. It was true she had an assignment to do over the Colonization Days break, but it was ten times more of a pain than anything a sixth-grader would have to do.

The assignment was to use the vacation time to write a report about a place in Church history other than Easterbury. The students who were leaving town to go on vacation or go home could just attend a service at a church in the places they were visiting and write up their thoughts, but to Kieli, who had no plans to leave Easterbury, the assignment was as good as a personal insult.

Insult or not, it wouldn't do her any good *not* to work on it. She looked up from the printout and pulled an old Church history textbook from the books lined up across her desk. A student who graduated a long time ago had left it there, and it had some detail on parts of history that had been erased from current textbooks. She couldn't expect much, but she started flipping through the pages, thinking there might be something of use.

Just then, "Hey, he makes me so mad. Let's play a little joke on him." Becca's face appeared in front of her, poking through the textbook from under the desk. "A joke?" Kieli asked, jumping back a little at the sudden appearance, her hand stopping mid-page-turn. Becca pulled herself out of the desk and knelt in front of Kieli (on top of the desk, of course).

"You saw the radio he had, right? The old beat-up one. It's possessed by something — an evil spirit radio. It's weird for someone to keep something like that so close," Becca said, putting the details of her own existence aside, and confidently proceeded to reveal her brilliant plan. "We'll take it away from him and lure him to the school. When he follows us here, we'll drop a rock or something on him from the roof and squash him flat. That'll show him."

". . . Wait a second, Becca. Look." Kieli sighed and held up a hand to interrupt her friend's monologue. Becca closed her mouth, but the expression on her face showed that she hadn't the slightest doubt that Kieli would agree to her plan. Kieli felt a prickling pain in her temples.

It was fundamentally wrong in every possible way. First of all, Kieli didn't really want to do this to begin with, and certain parts of how to carry this plan out, like how and where they would get such a rock and who would drop it, had been flung to the other side of the stars. Besides, however you thought about it, this was not a "little joke"–level prank.

"If we do that, he'll die." She felt she would get very tired explaining everything, so for now, she just pointed out the last problem. It should have been an extremely reasonable opinion. But Becca looked at her blankly and replied, as if it was obvious, that, "He wouldn't die from a little thing like that."

"Unbelievable. Look. A real, live person . . ." Kieli added to her explanation, thinking that perhaps Becca didn't understand because she was already dead.

But when she did, Becca beat her to the punch and added, "I mean, he's an Undying."

This struck Kieli speechless, and she stared back at Becca's determined blue eyes as she gazed directly at her.

". . . Undying . . . ?" was all she could finally say.

Becca nodded, very seriously, and said, "You didn't know? I thought if anyone would figure it out, you would, Kieli. I mean, he doesn't have a soul; it's just a rock moving a corpse around. . . . Hey, are you listening, Kieli? Why the scary face?"

"Oh, uh . . ." Kieli had started to think about something else for a second in the corner of her consciousness, but when Becca peered dubiously at her face, she cut off that line of thought. "I'm sorry. It's nothing," she murmured vaguely.

Becca tilted her head and blinked. "Kieli, could it be that you don't know about the Undying? Didn't they tell you when you were little, 'Church Soldiers will gouge your heart out'?"

"I know about them; I heard that all the time. But there's no way he could be an Undying. . . ." Kieli responded immediately, but the last part trailed off. If, for the sake of argument, the man from that afternoon really was an Undying, that would explain why she mistook him for a corpse when she saw him in front of the station.

Everyone on this planet, child or adult, knew that the Undying, otherwise known as "Demons of War," were monsters. Her grandmother wouldn't talk to her about those things very much, but a long time ago, a young aspiring author who lived in her apartment complex, among others, would make her listen to those stories until she got fed up with them.

Walking corpses, with perpetually moving power sources instead of hearts. It was said that at the end of the War, when the fighting had turned into such a quagmire that there was no hope of salvation and mankind was beginning to lose its humanity, the Undying were mass-produced, recycling the bodies of dead soldiers. They would never die or grow old, and no matter how many times they were killed, they would get up and slaughter until there was nothing left; she had even heard that they ate the tainted meat of those they killed and made it their own flesh. (Anyway, she heard all this from the aspiring author, so she didn't know how much was true and how much he had embellished.)

It was eighty years ago that the War finally came to a natural end after causing mass destruction across the entire planet. After that, the church conducted a large-scale Undying Hunt, and it was said that this brought about their extinction.

"Even if there were any left, they wouldn't be wandering around like normal in a place like this. I mean, they're moving corpses. You know, demons of war?" Kieli declared, in a firm tone this time, trying to convince herself more than Becca. But as a result, she ended up ruthlessly denying Becca's point, and as expected, Becca pouted, her feelings hurt.

"So we'll test him to see if he'll die or not. If he's an Undying, he won't die no matter what we do."

"What if he's a normal human?"

"If he dies, we'll know he was normal."

". . . . . ." Kieli furrowed her brow, feeling that their answers weren't meshing somehow. After thinking for a moment about *how* they weren't meshing, she let out an earnest sigh. She looked into Becca's eyes, through which she could faintly see the opposite wall, and said admonishingly, "Hey, do you understand what you're saying? That's not the way a living person would think."

"You think so?"

Because she said it in such a carefree way, it was hard to tell if she was playing dumb or if she really didn't understand. Kieli unintentionally took on a harsher tone and said, "Cut it out, Becca. You really are dead. A living human being would never think of anything so scary."

"What? You're not like normal girls either, Kieli. You can't even make living friends. I'm your only friend, Kieli."

"Don't just decide we're friends. You decided to haunt me on your own, Becca. To me, you're just a nuisance." She thought she might have gone too far after she said it, but Becca was a little mean herself, saying she couldn't make any living friends. Sometimes they had fights like this. Usually, they would both go too far, and it would be declared a draw due to injury on both sides.

But this time, an expression something like despair appeared unexpectedly on Becca's face.

"I never thought I'd hear you say something like that, Kieli . . ." Matching her fading voice, Becca's form disappeared from sight.

"Bec . . ." Her heart stopped for a second, but it wasn't as if Becca's presence had left the room. She was probably just sulking as usual. Kieli was sure she would pop up again soon enough.

Breathing another small sigh, Kieli looked back down to her textbook.

As she turned the pages without really looking at them, she started thinking about something different again — an experience from when she was little that she had pushed to the bottom of her memory.

It was a lie that the Undying had been wiped out — at least it was seven years ago. She had a feeling the man who died in front of her when she was seven was an Undying. Armored Church Soldiers chased him and killed him. His stone heart rolled out.

But after the incident, no matter how many times she asked her grandmother about it, she could never get her to say if she was right or wrong. She only told her that those things didn't exist anymore, and the topic naturally became one that was not to be touched on, inside her home or out of it. Her grandmother died the next spring, and Kieli, having no living relatives, was sent to the boarding school.

And yet there were so many more things she would have wanted to ask her grandmother if she were still alive. She didn't really question it when she was little, but why could she see the spirits of the dead? Did the father and mother she didn't remember have the same ability, or could it be that they abandoned her *because* of this creepy power? The one thing she did know, without even asking directly, was that her grandmother wasn't her real grandmother. The landlady of their apartment, a plump woman who loved gossip, spread it throughout the neighborhood. "This doesn't leave this room, but the old woman on the third floor took that girl in off the streets." Everyone in the apartment knew it pretty well for it not having left that room.

". . . Ugh, I can do it tomorrow." In the end, she lost the will to study and plopped her forehead down onto her textbook.

A small photograph on the open page caught her eye. It was a picture of an abandoned mine from before the War, and the Church history textbook treated it as a historic War ruin. A large number of ancient battlefields from the end of the War remained in the wilderness in the eastern region of Easterbury.

He said he was going east, she thought vaguely, remembering the man she had met that afternoon. The first person she had met other than herself who could see dead people. It's possible that he would give Kieli some of the answers she sought.

He didn't know how long it had been since the last time he had come to this town. At the time, the old station was new, but the town was just as bustling with the comings and goings of travelers as it was today. No, that was when they had finally reconstructed Easterbury after it was completely wasted as the final battlefield in the War, so maybe the people's faces were a few degrees livelier and more full of hope for the future back then. The old building wasn't an elaborate thing like the tasteless new station they had now — just a crude building of concrete and iron — but apparently it was out of proportion with the meaningless pomp of the day's architecture and the energy of the people using it.

As he leaned against the fence that went along the railroad track and lit a cigarette, he cast his gaze toward the square roof of the old station looming in the darkness, and old memories came flooding back.

"*Herbie.*" A staticky voice mixed with a slight prewar accent addressed him from near his feet.

"*Harvey*," he corrected for the hundredth time, and glared down at the small radio that he had left on the ground with his backpack. The guy possessing the radio no doubt died never having pronounced the "harv" sound in his lifetime, and as a result, he would skillfully pronounce it "herb," to the point where Harvey wondered if he was actually getting it wrong on purpose.

"*Hey. There's a little thing called 'tact.'*"

"What are we talking about now?"

"*Listen to me, damn it. This afternoon. That girl you left behind — you saw her face, didn't you? Looking like her parents had abandoned her. You didn't have to be so harsh.*"

Oh, that, Harvey thought, blowing smoke into the blue-gray night sky. "But it's such a pain dealing with living people," he muttered, half to himself.

"*No one's asking if it's a pain for you or not. Damn it, man, it's like you left the words 'patience' and 'consideration' behind somewhere in your lifetime.*"

"Well, I have lived a long time."

"If you've lived such a long time, you should have polished up your damn humanity."

A small, unpleasant, booming sound resonated from the speaker when the radio spat the words, and Harvey ducked his head and averted his eyes, as if looking to run away. Why should he have to be lectured on humanity by a *radio*?

As his eyes wandered, he noticed someone's shadow and lightly kicked the radio with his toe to shut it up. On the other side of the street, under a dull yellow streetlight that flickered nervously, sat an old woman, so thin and frail that he couldn't distinguish her from the rags she was wearing. It was already deep into the night, and even if it hadn't been, there wouldn't be many people who would have had business on the rusty old streets along the train track. She was probably a vagrant who had taken up residence in the area.

The old woman scrutinized him with her small, olive-brown eyes and slightly opened lips that were almost one with her wrinkles.

Her voice was so completely withered that he couldn't make it out right away, but after a second, he understood that she had called to him, "You're an Undying, aren't you?" The call startled him for just a moment, but he immediately relaxed his guard and let out a sigh mixed with a wry laugh.

"I hate that old people can figure it out so easily. I guess weird senses get sharper when you don't have much time left."

"Have you come to take this old senile crone away? The nights are getting harder and harder; I would be happier if I passed on before the winter came."

"I'm not a grim reaper, you know."

"Oh yes. I know . . ." the old woman laughed in a dry voice; her fingers, falling listlessly at her side like dried twigs, convulsed slightly. Raising those fingers just a little, as if even that simple task took tremendous effort, she said, "Take my hand . . ."

Harvey hesitated, but the radio quietly urged him, *"Go to her,"* so he reluctantly left his things and walked toward the old woman. He knelt down, took the aged, shrunken hand, and held it lightly. It was a parched and small hand and seemed as if it would crumble into cinders if he held it any tighter.

"My hands have turned altogether ugly and useless over these eighty years, but your hands don't change, do they? Such beautiful hands . . ." The old woman closed her eyes as if to make sure of the feeling in her hand and exhaled contentedly.

"I was just a small child back then, but I still remember it clearly. Watching the video transmission of the dashing parade in honor of your troops' triumphant return, people waving flags in praise as they greeted you. Back then, people were still calling you the saviors of war."

"That was a long time ago. I didn't think there was anyone left that remembered."

"Yes, our generation has just about died out. Now you are the only ones who can tell the world how foolish that War was . . ."

The old woman stopped there, and the silence strangely amplified the creaking of the rusty fence isolating the railroad tracks as it caught the wind.

After a little while, Harvey realized that those were the old woman's last words. The small, emaciated body had become a dried-out husk, no more than skin and bones.

". . . Hey, don't go making it my job to hand down history."

His voice would most likely no longer reach the old woman's ears, but he felt like griping anyway and cursed at her quietly. He had met too many people who would say whatever the hell they wanted, force their dying will onto him, and then go off and die. *You may be all satisfied that it's over for you, but try thinking about how I feel, having every damn thing forced on me.*

Still grumbling inwardly, he took the old woman's other drooping hand as carefully as he could and laid both hands on her knees, one on top of the other. "Don't you come haunting me," he ordered, before closing his eyes and offering a silent prayer.

Just then, *"Herbie!"* the radio shouted, with the crunching of heavy static. " — !" His face snapped up, and, as a reflex, he turned around, getting ready to defend himself — but the next moment, he froze, still only half standing.

There was a small girl standing beside the backpack he had left by the fence. With her wide-collared black bolero jacket and her black skirt, her all-black figure melted like a shadow into the darkness, but that only served to emphasize how out of place a girl like her was in a place like this at this time of night.

She was the girl from the boarding school that he had met at the new station on the other side of town that afternoon, the girl who could see spirits.

In the instant before he could think how to react, the girl bent down and very casually picked up the radio by its string.

"Don't touch me!"

Hearing the radio's overblown objection, he understood, too late, the meaning behind her action. The girl turned and started to run, the radio hanging from one hand.

"Wait!!"

After a second, Harvey hurried after the girl. She was close enough that if he tried, he could catch her without any problem, but she took advantage of her small physique to slip through a narrow break in the fence and escape to the railroad side.

"Hey, what are you thinking!?" he yelled at the girl's back, forcing his body to squeeze through the opening. It looked like it was made for a cat or something; of course there was no way a big man like him could fit through.

Running along the railroad track, the girl glanced back at him.

When he saw her face, Harvey started and froze in spite of himself. Overlapping the form of the black-haired girl, he could see the face of a different, blond girl. It was the ghost that had been haunting the black-haired girl. He wouldn't call her dangerous, but there was something decidedly different about her than when he had seen her that afternoon: her gruesome appearance, with a half-sunken head through which he could see her shattered skull.

The two overlapping girls snickered together. It was a strange, twisted smile.

With a faint vibration, two round lights appeared far down the tracks. Only a freight train would be running at this time of night. The girl's black uniform cut a clear silhouette against the center of the light, like a shadow sewn onto a white wall.

The girl stopped and, holding the radio up with both hands, shouted in a voice loud enough to be heard over the oncoming train.

"Hey, the Undying don't die, right? Even if they're hit by a train?" She was using the black-haired girl's voice, but most likely it was the ghost who was talking. "*I* died. Did you know that? I was hit by a train and died!"

Like hell I'd know that, Harvey swore inwardly, and spitting, "Damn it, get out of the way!" to the innocent fence, he forced his body out of the opening in the wire mesh. A piece of wire that was poking out in an inconvenient direction stabbed the palm of his hand, but this wasn't the time to let that bother him.

The headlights and thunderous roar of the train were approaching. The girl raised the radio above her head and waved it toward the train tracks.

Just then, a human shadow rose out like smoke from the radio that she was about to throw and grabbed the ghost girl's arm, as if trying to take her down with him.

"Kyaa, what is this!?" the ghost girl screamed, struggling. The moment she did, the radio slipped out of her hand and hit the rail with a clang. Following suit, the tangible girl fell over and landed on the tracks.

"Argh, what are you doing, Corporal?" Harvey chided, finally free of the fence, and ran to them at full speed.

First he picked up the girl's body and tossed her, far from gently, to the side of the track. He immediately turned back and went for the radio. His foot got caught in the ballast but, after nearly falling over, he somehow managed to grab hold of the radio's cord in one hand, and then —

Hoooonk!

The horn pierced his eardrums with a shrill noise resembling an explosion, and the two headlights, rushing forward as if to relieve some stress, filled his vision.

The white lights brought with them a shock wave that gave him the sensation that they had run his body through. Before he could make out which of the girls screamed, his sense of hearing flew off somewhere.

What did I do?

Kieli wore a sullen expression as she puzzled it over, restlessly moving her breakfast of soggy cereal to her mouth.

It was true that she had her stupid moments, but she wanted to think that it wasn't so terminal that she would get into bed having mistaken her uniform for sleepwear. She had gone to bed sulking last night, and when she opened her eyes, she was in bed wearing her uniform. Of course it had gotten all wrinkled, and when she went to change clothes, her day already off to a gloomy start, she discovered that, while it didn't stand out because the fabric was black, the uniform was covered in dirt, and it was even soaked through with blackish stains that looked like blood. Startled, she lifted her skirt to see that both her knees were scraped, and the instant she noticed they started to sting — but those were no more than scratches, and it would seem that the stains were not of her own blood.

Becca still hadn't appeared since vanishing the night before.

What did I do?

She unconsciously let out a small groan and tilted her head. When she did, she hit the back of it on the corner of someone's tray as they passed behind her.

"Ow . . ."

It happened so suddenly she was more dazed than angry as she turned around to see freckle-faced Zilla put down her tray to sit a little ways off and start chatting with her roommate. There was no way she could not have noticed bumping into Kieli, but whatever; it would have been creepy if she'd apologized anyway.

Kieli stayed quiet and focused on finishing her own breakfast. She had no interest in Zilla and her roommate's boring conversation, but their voices reached one ear despite her lack of attention.

The first thing they got worked up about was something so incredibly trivial as how many different pairs of glasses Miss Hanni had. Next they brought up the subject of a railroad accident that happened at the old station very early that morning. It was the first time Kieli learned that anything like that had taken place.

"Apparently an animal jumped out in front of a freight train and got hit. They're saying it was a cat."

"What do you mean 'they're saying'?"

Zilla raised her nose at her roommate's naive question, as if to emphasize that she had all the answers. "They couldn't find the body of the animal that got hit, and in the end, the railway department settled it by saying it was a cat and started the trains running again. But don't you think it's weird? That there wouldn't be a body anywhere." When she got to that point, she suddenly lowered her voice and brought her nose right up to her roommate. "Like maybe someone picked up the dead cat and took it home to use in a demonic ritual."

Kieli felt the cruel glances they sent in her direction, but she ignored them, letting them brush past her cheeks. Based on something she'd happened to overhear recently, apparently there was gossip going around that Becca's voice, the one that had chased out her roommate last spring, was Kieli chanting demonic incantations.

She ate her bland cereal quickly, without tasting it, and left her seat. Zilla and her roommate were still laughing behind her, but she didn't turn around once as she cleaned up her dishes and left the cafeteria. Outside, she took a deep breath, then abruptly broke into a full run down the hall.

After a sequence of actions consisting of running to her room, opening the door, going inside, and closing it, she yelled, "Becca!" as loud as she could without having it leak into the hall.

Becca didn't show herself right away, but when Kieli's firm voice demanded again, "I know you're here," she gradually appeared on her top bunk, as usual. Kieli turned a sharp gaze on her from where she stood in front of the door.

"Were you at the railroad track last night? What were you doing? Did that blood come from a cat?" It was obvious that

Becca had used Kieli's body without asking while she was asleep, so she didn't bother asking that.

"A cat?" Becca asked, looking blank. From her attitude, it seemed that she really had no recollection of a cat, so Kieli pressed, "Then where did the blood come from?" For a moment, the look on Becca's face seemed to say, "Oops!" and then she suddenly answered, in all seriousness, "That's right. It was a cat."

Kieli glared fixedly back at her and repeated, "Where did the blood come from?"

". . . . ." Becca stayed silent for a while, but, resigning herself to her undaunted roommate's threatening attitude, she finally confessed slowly, "I was testing him. To see if he wouldn't die. Because you wouldn't believe me, Kieli."

It wasn't as though Kieli hadn't anticipated that, but when she heard it, her vision went black for a second. *Then it wasn't a cat that was hit by that cargo train; it was something much bigger — a grown man?*

"Then what . . . what happened after that? Did he live?"

"I don't know."

"You don't *know*? You didn't check?"

"I was scared, so I came home. I mean, when the train ran into him . . . there was a 'splat' . . . A 'splat' sound. It really sounded like that."

"Of course it did!"

Her tone intensified as she got more irritated. Becca recoiled on top of the bed and said, "Well . . . well, I didn't know it would be so scary. Did that happen to me, too? Was I squashed like that, too? Is that what I looked like? What do I look like to you, Kieli?"

As Kieli watched, the beautiful face, hanging down like it was about to cry, began to dissolve. She could see the skin melt away, exposing the flesh and bone.

"Becca . . ." Kieli couldn't scold her anymore. It was like the girl who had been hit by a train and killed two years ago had finally learned exactly how terrible her death was after seeing the same thing happen to someone else.

"It's okay. I understand. You wait here and stay out of trouble. I'll go look for him," Kieli said over her shoulder.

Still, that didn't excuse Becca's actions, and on top of it all, depending on how things went, Kieli could be accused of murder. Kieli gave up on Becca and ran out of the room.

The railroad tracks formed a half-circle around the southern edge of town, and went on through to the wilderness that spread to the east and west. The new station stood on the western side of town, and the closed-down old station stood on the eastern side. Before the switch to the new station, the east side flourished as the town's center, but now no evidence of that remained, and the area had become a deserted ghost town.

The railroad's accident investigation team had already cleared out, but it was easy to find where the incident had taken place. Part of the tall fence that followed the railroad track was broken, and she could see that extreme emergency measures had been taken by the wires that were a different color in that one spot.

No one was there from the railroad, but instead, the Church's corpse disposal team was on the scene. The corpse disposal unit was the lowest rank of priests in the Church, and the two men wearing the team's gray robes did not appear to take any pride in their work as they expressionlessly carried a body on a sheet of galvanized steel.

Kieli's heart pounded as she pretended to walk casually by and stole a look at the body's face. It was someone else — the dried husk of an old woman. Feeling some relief that it was not the person she was looking for, she passed by the body, then stopped and looked back. *Probably a vagrant who couldn't make it through the night. It was cold last night.* Closing her eyes just a little, she offered a prayer for the old woman and watched as they took her body away.

The corpse disposal team's pace didn't change at all as they walked away, heading west along the tracks.

Kieli didn't know how long it had been there, but the spirit of the old woman was kneeling above her remains and looking in her direction. It wasn't as if anyone was watching, but Kieli kept her hand at her side as she gave a small wave good-bye.

The old woman raised her hand slowly, too. Kieli thought she was going to wave back, but instead, she extended a bony index finger and pointed. She followed the direction indicated with her eyes and saw, at the end of the tracks, on the easternmost end of town where the ruined buildings stopped, the square roof of the old station.

When she returned her gaze to ask what it meant, the old woman's spirit had disappeared.

Entrance into the station was prohibited, but Kieli snuck in through a chink in the iron fence. Four gray concrete walls formed the inside of the building, which was gloomy and cold, despite it being midmorning. As she looked around, Kieli shivered and regretted having forgotten her coat.

It had been abandoned for years, but there was a surprising amount of luggage strewn around the building. Kieli had the impression that it just been left there like that because it cost too much to dispose of old things. The ticket barrier leading to the platform stood directly across from her. Broken benches and pieces of iron lay piled in the waiting area to her left, and to her right was the now glassless window to the station attendants' room, its "Employees Only" sign hanging at a slant.

The stagnant air and silence drifted through the atmosphere as if time had stopped there many years ago.

Faint voices escaped from inside the waiting area. She found herself holding her breath as she headed in that direction. A few rows of rusty iron benches that apparently had been used on the platform formed an unnatural pile in front of the waiting area. She could hear the voices from the other side of the unstable iron wall.

When she stuck her face between a space in the benches to see the other side, the first thing she saw was the back of a copper-colored head.

"There's no need to hurry. How long are you gonna whine over staying *one* extra day? You're pretty old yourself. Get yourself some more composure."

Even before she heard the way he easily let such biting remarks leave his mouth, she could tell the back belonged to the traveler who called himself Harvey. He leaned back on one of the three-person benches used for the waiting area and rested his crossed legs on the bench across from him.

Oh. He's fine . . .

Kieli almost fell down on the spot as the worries that had built up inside her came crumbling down. Becca's testimony had been a lie all along, and it must have really been a cat that got hit. But she did feel bad for the cat.

"Shut up!! I shouldn't have to deal with you treating me like an old man." A man's voice jumped abruptly from the radio that had been placed on the bench by his feet. She gaped for a second and then remembered that Becca had said that a ghost possessed the radio.

"Damn it, if things had gone the way they were supposed to,

we'd be there in three days! But now we can't move until you stop looking like you came straight out of a ghost story."

"Oh, shut up. Like it's my fault. If you don't stop complaining, I'll cut your power."

"You're not gonna throw me away somewhere and run off while my power's off, are you?"

"I wouldn't do that. I promised I'd take you to the mine, didn't I? Am I that untrustworthy?"

"Trust is something you build up through your daily actions."

Every time the voice came from the speaker, particles like blackish static spat out around it, forming a blurry human face, and then dispersing when the voice stopped. Kieli couldn't help staring at the static particles as they gathered and ran away like microbes. She had never seen a spirit like that before.

The static clustered together and formed the human face again. The face, composed of strange greenish-black particles, was dark, like a shadow had fallen over it, so she couldn't tell for sure, but it seemed to be the face of a man with sunken cheeks. When the outlines of the face were almost complete, green particles would go on to form eyeball-like spheres in the hollow eye sockets.

And those eyes suddenly turned and glared in her direction. Kieli stiffened at the sudden movement, and before she could react, Harvey demanded, "Who's there?" He sprang from the bench and turned around; behind him, the staticky face opened its mouth angrily. *"Little girl, don't you ever learn!?"* it yelled, at the same time emitting a mass of sound from the speakers that transformed into a shock wave and attacked her. Knocked back by the lump of invisible air, Kieli fell on her rear. Immediately, the already unstable wall of piled benches gave a sudden lurch. She didn't scream because she forgot to use her voice, and while she was at it, she also failed to remember to run away. Still on the ground, she looked up above her. The iron benches came clattering down. . . .

There was a dull *thunk!* sound. Someone's arm had caught the bench, getting between it and her in the nick of time, and thanks to the arm, Kieli's head went unsmashed.

"Tsk . . ." Harvey clicked his tongue and pushed the thick, heavy iron bench away with his right elbow, clearly irked. Glancing at Kieli's face as she sat there dumbstruck, he turned around and shouted back to the radio, "Calm down, Corporal. It wasn't her. There's no one inside her now!"

When she saw the side of his face, Kieli's breath stopped.

The skin on the left half of his face had been torn off from his temple to his cheek, and crushed blood vessels and muscle tissue showed through in a mottled reddish-black pattern. On the arm opposite the one that caught the bench, his coat sleeve was torn to shreds, and his lower arm barely hung on to the upper half by naked muscle fibers.

"Nooooo!" This time, Kieli screamed.

"Oh, just shut up. This is partially your fault, you know," Harvey spat at Kieli, twisting the unharmed half of his face in annoyance as she screamed in his ear. "Corporal, listen!" he yelled again at the radio. The spirit in the radio spun a whirlwind of static as it now formed not only a face, but an entire body, in midair. He was still a fuzzy gathering of particles, but Kieli could tell that he was wearing a brimmed hat over his eyes and a military uniform. The lower half of one of his legs disappeared at the knee, as if melting into the air.

The static soldier moved his gaze sluggishly to the left and right, and his green eyeballs glinted in her direction — he'd finally found her. Maybe he was trying to shout something; his jaw dropped to a normally impossible angle. He tried to take a step toward her with his lost foot, but, as there was no foot there, he stumbled and almost fell — the kind of thing, Kieli thought, that shouldn't have affected a ghost.

Kieli felt sick, not because his form was so terrifying, but because of his bizarre behavior.

When the soldier opened wide his pitch-dark mouth, a low groaning sound came from the speaker and shook the air. The scattered benches convulsed noisily across the floor, and a few of them rose into the air like marionettes.

"Corp — damn it, it's no use, he can't hear me," Harvey spat with a click of his tongue, and immediately afterward one of the benches found its target and came at them. "We're getting out of here!" With his good right arm (though there must have been at least a crack in it after the bench fell on it), Harvey took Kieli's hand and ran outside of the waiting area.

"Why do you have to have such bad timing!? He almost killed me with that temper once, you know!"

"I didn't know — but . . . but how are you still alive?"

Kieli moved her feet forward almost as if they were falling as he dragged her along. She couldn't understand even half of what was going on. No matter how she looked at it, someone in Harvey's condition would be dead, or at least, they wouldn't be able to move around normally with those injuries.

A bench flew past, grazing by the two as they ran from the waiting area, and Kieli's feet became tangled as she drew back in surprise. "Wah!" She dragged Harvey down with her, and they both tumbled and rolled along the cold station floor.

"You're in the way! Get outside! Why do I always —"

Thrust violently aside, Kieli had scrambled on all fours to a few steps away when she heard the dull *thunk* sound of something getting hit behind her; and Harvey's caustic words were abruptly cut off.

". . . . . . ?" As a reflex, she stopped moving and nervously looked back.

A flying bench had crashed into the "Employees Only" sign, causing the door to cave in — Harvey was between the bench and the door. The seat of the iron bench had run deeply into his throat, like the blade of a guillotine.

His copper-colored eyes open wide, Harvey, pinned to the door, had stopped moving completely.

Only half-standing and twisting her neck in an unnatural angle, Kieli stared blankly at the dead, pinned body. Her thought processes had short-circuited, and she couldn't react immediately to the voice she suddenly heard in her head saying, "Kieli, look out!"

Immediately her body started moving on its own, like it was being pulled by strings, and made a very nice dive out of the way. The bench that had come at her hit the ground where she had just been and was smashed into a grotesque shape.

Thrown to the ground, for just a second, she could see another pair of legs overlapping her own, and a blond girl slid out of her. "I'm sorry, Kieli. I'm sorry." Kneeling like a scolded child, Becca floated in front of Kieli, repeating her apology over and over.

"I didn't think it would turn into this. I'm sorry, Kieli."

"Becca, I —"

She was about to say, "I'm fine, but Harvey-san . . ." as a beastly roar thundered from inside the waiting area.

"*You!*" the one-legged soldier shouted upon seeing Becca, and a shock wave shot out of the speaker, accompanied by a grating dissonance.

"*Kyaaaa!*"

Becca took a direct hit and disappeared with a scream. "No, Becca!" Kieli automatically reached out in an effort to grab hold of Becca. But her hands only grabbed empty space, and the force of the shock wave sent her head over heels into the wall. Just before she hit it, Harvey, still pinned to the door, thrust his arm to the side and worked as a cushion.

"Har —" Kieli looked beside her in surprise, when the radio's speaker strummed out a still more terrible, grating noise. She impulsively drew her head back and returned her gaze to the waiting area.

The soldier's figure wavered for an instant and then disappeared suddenly, like when a video signal turns off.

A wisp of black smoke rose from the radio. Apparently it had shorted out.

Save for the small pattering sound of the dust settling back to the floor, silence returned to the station.

"Are you satisfied, Corporal?" Harvey grumbled beside a dazed Kieli, pulling the bench out of his throat. The bench fell to the ground with a clang, and Harvey kicked it with the bottom of his shoe, as if yelling at it to go away. Kieli gaped at the effortlessness of his actions, but panic set in after a while, and she cried, "Are, er, are you okay? We need a doctor!"

Unsure whether it would be better to take him with her or bring someone to him, she looked desperately back and forth from Harvey to the exit. But he ignored her frenzy and casually said, "It's fine. Leave it alone; it'll close up," as if nothing was wrong (although he used a scratchy voice that made her wonder if the bench had torn his vocal cords, and coughed violently a few times as if he was in some pain).

"You're . . . okay . . . ?"

She sat down next to him and took a long, hard look at the wound. What she saw was a thick black liquid resembling coal tar oozing out of his blood and wrapping around the severed tissue like a living thing. She leaned forward to see what it was, but Harvey covered his throat with one hand.

"Um, are you really an Undying . . . ?" she asked, looking at his face with upturned eyes.

Harvey, for his part, blinked in surprise. "Huh? I thought you already knew. Didn't your buddy tell you?"

"Oh yeah, Becca!" His question reminded Kieli of Becca, and she passed her gaze hastily over her surroundings. "Becca, are you okay? Where are you?"

Her "buddy" didn't answer.

"Becca . . . ?"

When the terrifying thought hit her that Becca might actually have been completely erased, she heard a muttered, "That scared me. . . ." Becca floated into view in front of Kieli with a somewhat pale expression. "A little more and that would have killed me . . ."

"You're already dead," Kieli shot back, in shock. Then, feeling the situation was somehow funny, she let out a small laugh. Becca said, "Oh yeah. I am dead, aren't I?" and laughed bashfully, and the two put their faces together and giggled.

". . . You two seem to be enjoying yourselves. I feel like you've caused nothing but trouble for me, though."

She didn't really know why herself, but when Harvey leaned against the collapsed door and let out a sigh of complete exhaustion, her eyes filled with tears, perhaps from relief, and before she knew it she was crying and laughing at the same time.

A bell rang noisily, announcing the departure of the eastbound train.

"Kieli, Kieli, we're leaving!" Becca announced excitedly, kneeling on her seat with her face against the window like a small child.

"I know. Wait a minute." Kieli was reaching up and pushing her shoulder bag onto the overhead shelf. It only contained a few days' worth of clothes and a reference book, but that reference book was insanely heavy. She shouldn't have brought it.

She somehow managed to stow her luggage and, holding the coat she'd taken off, sat down next to Becca. After agonizing over which of her personal wardrobe — which wasn't very large to begin with — to wear, in the end she wore the black school-designated coat and her uniform. She got a stern look from Becca, who appeared in her favorite red coat, asking, "What is with that drab outfit?" But ostensibly she was on a trip for a school assignment, so she felt like wearing her uniform was the right thing to do.

I'm going on a train trip to write my Church history report. I'll be back before the Colonization holidays are over. She wrote her notice of leave, and, taking advantage of Miss Hanni, the teacher on duty, being away from her office, she left it on her desk without a word. Her grandmother had left her a little bit of money, and she planned to use that to pay for her trip. There was never a pressing need for it in her dull daily life at the boarding school, so this was the first time she ever wanted to use the money.

Her destination was the abandoned mines in eastern Easterbury, one of the War ruins. A full day had passed since the commotion at the old station yesterday, and it was already the third day of the Colonization Days break, but she should be able to make the round-trip within the remaining week.

The fact that the history of the War was part of Church history and therefore within the parameters of the assignment was just an excuse (of course, she did plan on writing the report, too), but the biggest factor in her decision was that she had heard that *they* were heading for the abandoned mines.

Sitting in the boxed seat opposite her was the young man

with copper-colored hair. He was sitting cross-legged on the seat with his shoes still on and had been fiddling with parts of the broken radio, but when he noticed Kieli's gaze, he looked up and frowned in obvious annoyance. "Hey, would you stop following me?"

"We just happen to be going to the same place," Kieli answered plainly.

"Jinx . . ." Harvey cursed to himself, returning his gaze to the radio.

Surprisingly, the wounds on the left side of his body that were so terrible yesterday had already healed to the point where, today, they were no more than inflamed scars on his skin. His neck apparently hadn't recovered yet; he hid his wound by zipping his thick parka closed all the way to his chin. The coat he was wearing yesterday had been torn to shreds, and the parka was a spare he had stuffed in his backpack. Sometimes he stuck his fingers in his collar like it was bothering him.

Harvey was a legendary Undying — the first person Kieli had met who could see the spirits of the dead like she could. She wanted to follow him and talk to him a little more, even if it was only during the holidays. It was that thought that caused her to set out on a weeklong train trip — a very bold move considering her normal life.

It was kind of funny to think that she, the weirdest girl at the boarding school, was the most normal one in this group. Her ability to come up with such opinions was probably evidence that she wasn't normal, but Kieli somehow felt comfortable in these circumstances. With these people, Kieli didn't need to hide her weird power like she did at school.

The departure bell stopped. After a moment of silence and a slight jolt, the train started to move.

"Wow, it's moving!" Kieli squealed automatically, leaning toward the window next to Becca. The scene on the platform, the white palms of people waving good-bye to family and lovers, slid quietly past.

"Having fun, Kieli?" Becca asked suddenly, gazing outside with her face lined up next to Kieli's.

"Yes." Kieli nodded half-consciously, still staring at the platform as it flowed away.

"Oh good, then I feel better," Becca murmured, in a somehow resolved tone. "Um, you know? The truth is, I think I've known since the accident the day before yesterday. I died like that a long, long time ago. I stopped existing here before I even met you, Kieli. So I can't stay here and play forever, you know? I might go crazy like that soldier's spirit and hurt you one day."

"What is this all of a sudden?" Kieli asked, pulling her gaze away from the platform, her eyes wide. Becca ignored her question and turned her ever-mischievous smile to Harvey in the opposite seat.

"Harvey, I'm leaving Kieli to you. Take responsibility and make sure to look after her. She's very shy, and she's never followed anyone on her own initiative like this before. I followed her around because she would have been hopeless without me. But only because she needed me! And I guess I should apologize. Sorry for causing you so much trouble."

Harvey looked up in some surprise, and mumbled, "Oh, it was nothing." He looked at Becca, and a complex expression showed on his face for a split second, but in the end, he turned back to the radio on his lap without a word. "Becca, what are you saying . . . ?" Kieli cut in, panicking at having suddenly been entrusted to someone else, but ". . . Becca?"

Suddenly, sparkling white lights were surrounding Becca.

"You'll be fine without me now, Kieli," she said, smiling brightly. Her face turned into particles of soft light and gradually began to fade. Her gentle voice rang deep in Kieli's ears.

"Thank you. It was fun being with you. I want you to have lots more fun after this. Because you still have a long future ahead of you, Kieli. . . ."

The specks of light slowly melted into the air and disappeared; by the time the train left the platform, Becca was no longer on board.

Kieli stared blankly at the now-empty seat next to her for a long time. Her heart was empty, and she didn't know what kind of face she should make. Her gaze slowly wandered to the opposite seat, and her eyes met with Harvey's; he had stopped fixing the radio and was looking her way.

"Why . . . ?" The instant she spoke, tears came to her eyes, and she couldn't say any more.

"She came to terms with it. People who have died disappear. It's only natural," the legendary Undying told Kieli in a calm, quiet voice, his copper-colored eyes fixed in cold inexpression. Then he went right back to his work, but, perhaps feeling a need to say more, he added haltingly, "Why not see her off without crying? She said she had fun, didn't she?"

Kieli looked wordlessly back out the car window, and pressed her lips firmly together, holding back her tears. If that was the path Becca had decided was best, the least Kieli could do as a farewell gift was to see her off without crying. Becca was selfish and annoying, but she was the best roommate Kieli had ever had, and her first good friend. It wasn't true that she hadn't existed anymore after her death. At the very least, to Kieli, Becca was more sure to be by her side than any classmate Kieli had ever had.

Under the sand-colored sky, the scenery outside the window changed to the streets of Easterbury and passed on by as if nothing had happened. A single tear slid down her cheek. She wiped it away with the palm of her hand, as she stared fixedly, almost in a glare, at the passing streets.

CHAPTER 2

MAY I SEE YOUR TICKET?

She felt the cool air inside a tunnel. Countless dead bodies lay in heaps around her; Kieli stood in their center. Some had their throats slashed, some had their abdomens blown away by gunshots, some had swords sticking out of their backs. Most of them were already corpses, but there were some who soon would be. Those who could move walked over the corpses, desperately carrying their injured, exhausted limbs forward before they succumbed to gravity, aiming for the tunnel's exit.

Kieli had become one of the soldiers.

She lent a shoulder to a badly wounded comrade as she dragged her own body, now missing a leg. When they were only a few steps away from the exit, a sword was thrust violently into her companion's back. Supporting the weight of her collapsing friend, she turned around; behind her stood the "enemy." His face was blurry, and she couldn't make it out, but the one thing that impressed her was his blank expression, showing no sign of emotion. Without the slightest change in that expression, the "enemy" pulled the sword out of her friend's back, releasing a powerful spray of blood.

Kieli yelled something, and before she knew it, she had pointed the black gun in her hands toward the "enemy" and fired. The shot blew away the side of her opponent's head and one of his eyes. But the opponent merely scowled slightly, shook his head in annoyance, and, turning his blood-soaked sword, slashed at her effortlessly, as if it was a conditioned response that had permeated his spinal cord.

"Wah —"

She opened her eyes, surprised at her own cry.

She looked around, unable to remember where she was for a second. She was in a rectangular space that stretched narrowly before and behind her. The dim morning light penetrated the windows, spaced evenly along both walls, and she kept feeling a slight, regular vibration under her rear as she sat on a seat that was not particularly soft.

Music played from an old-fashioned radio on the window-sill at a low volume, only loud enough to fill the boxed seats where Kieli sat with her company. The music was mixed with terrible static, as if it was coming from very far away, and it was a type of music Kieli had never heard before.

"This is a song from a long time ago. It's called rock."

She heard a low voice coming from the speaker over the music.

"The Church forbids it, saying it's savage or something, but guerilla radio stations play it in secret."

"So there used to be different kinds of music besides Church music before the War?" Kieli asked in a quiet voice to match the speaker's volume, and the radio told her yes.

"There were lots of different kinds. And a lot of different value systems. Of all of them, I like rock the best. Those are songs that are about living through your own power."

"Hmmm . . ."

Kieli put her head against the cold glass of the window and gazed absently outside, turning an ear to the up-tempo melody that played faintly. She wasn't the best singer and didn't have a pretty voice, so she hated singing in the choir, but she felt like she might learn to like this music.

She found herself thinking, "I wish Becca could have heard this." Becca, with her bright, clear soprano voice and perfect pitch, was the most wonderful singer of hymns Kieli knew, but she actually seemed to have ten times more fun when she joked around singing parodies than when she was singing the boring hymns. She would be so happy to learn that the world had fun, free music like this and not just hymns.

Under the sky, dotted with thin, sand-colored clouds, the train continued its course along its track through the vast wilderness. Becca had said good-bye immediately after they left the Easterbury station, and for one reason or another, conversation was sparse as they passed the night on the train. Now it was the next morning.

Now that she thought of it, she had had a dream. Could it be that the soldier who refused to give up, who kept walking on his own even after losing a leg, was the Corporal . . . ?

"Corporal" was what Harvey called him, and apparently it was the rank he had achieved before dying in the War. He had died on the Easterbury battlefield in the final stages of the War, and the radio he possessed had made its way to a town very far away, where Harvey happened to pick it up, and they were on their way to where his physical remains slept. Or, that was the gist of their journey that Kieli had been able to figure out from their bits of conversation on the train.

Still facing outside the window, Kieli cast a sidelong glance at Harvey as he sat diagonally across from her. He leaned deeply into his seat, resting his crossed legs on the one next to Kieli's. Whether their conversation registered in his ears or not, his gaze was fixed diagonally downward, and he hadn't moved an inch for a long time. It was no wonder Kieli had mistaken him for a corpse when she first saw him in front of Easterbury Station; when Harvey wasn't doing anything, he stopped moving completely, as if he really was dead.

The skin on his left cheek, though scarred the day before, was almost perfectly healed now that one more night had passed. It would seem that the legend that said that he would get up again and again, no matter how many times he was killed, as long as he didn't lose the power source in his heart, wasn't an exaggeration. It was hard to believe right away that this man who seemed no older than a college student was in the War eighty years ago, just like the spirit in the radio, but it must be true — this was something she heard from the radio the night before. Harvey never participated in their conversations anyway, but it was a given that whenever the War got brought up, he would look clearly unhappy and pretend to be asleep.

"What?" Harvey asked, raising his downcast gaze slightly.

This took Kieli off guard; she opened and closed her mouth a few times, and answered, "Nothing. I was just looking," giving a reason that wasn't really a reason. At some point she had stopped just looking sideways at him — she was leaning forward and staring him in the face. Of course he'd wonder what she was doing.

He glared at her suspiciously, and Kieli pulled her head back.

"*Herbie*," the radio called out, as if throwing her a life preserver.

"That's *Harvey*," Harvey corrected him, sending his gaze toward the radio, his eyes only half open.

"*History homework is right up your alley. Even more so if it's Church history — you could tell her more than she'd ever want to know. You should just help her already.*"

"You're kidding. Why should I?" Harvey retorted immediately, scowling. The radio was clearly pretending he couldn't hear him when he answered Kieli's, "Really?" instead.

"*He's wandered all over the planet for decades since the War ended. If he didn't learn a lot about history, then he's just plain stupid. And while he's at it, he could tell you what kinds of filthy tricks the Church has been playing behind the scenes since the War —* "

"Aaahh!" Harvey yelled, a bit slow to interrupt the radio. He ran his eyes over the other box seats in the car, wearing an expression that said going on would cause trouble. He lowered his voice and said, "Shut up, you piece of scrap. You wanna make me a traitor to the Church?"

"*Why care* now?"

"I don't care; I just want to spend the time I have left in

peace. Anyway, a report like that, you should just write whatever'd make the Church happy and get your grade." Talking like a normal upperclassman, the legendary Undying, the Demon of War, laid the subject to rest and pulled a cigarette out of a pocket in his work pants.

Looking alternately from one face to the other (though, to be accurate, one of them didn't have a face), and listening to them argue, Kieli remembered one of the questions she thought Harvey might have the answer to. Her grandmother had told her never to speak of it in front of people at Church or school, but she thought it would be okay to ask Harvey.

"Um, hey. Harvey, have you noticed that there's no God in the Church?"

"What are you talking about? Have I *noticed* . . . ?"

As Harvey brought a lighter to his cigarette, he turned only his eyes toward her and furrowed his brow, but he didn't deny it. Rather, he seemed to be wondering why she would be asking about something so obvious. Kieli automatically brightened.

"Do you know why that is? I think this planet was too far away, so He went back home," she went on enthusiastically. This time, Harvey's expression seemed genuinely confused as he held the lighter, still lit, in front of his face. His cigarette fell out of his gaping mouth.

"You know. When the Saints who made the Church left their home planet and took God with them."

Kieli thought there must be something wrong with the way she'd asked and tried to explain further, when a stocky silhouette arrived and stood beside her seat.

She broke off and looked up to see a man in a dark blue uniform standing in the aisle. There were two rows of beautiful gold buttons running from its neatly closed, high collar to the hem above his knees. It was a railroad conductor's uniform like the ones Kieli aspired to wear, just a little, when she was a little girl. (The kids in her Sunday school class made fun of her, saying a girl could never be a conductor, and her dream was easily shattered.)

"Oh."

She hurriedly pulled a slightly bent ticket out of her skirt pocket and offered it to the conductor. The conductor leaned over and peered at the ticket, then smiled as if to say, "You're okay." His kind, gentle smile reminded Kieli of her childhood dream, and she smiled bashfully back at him.

While Kieli put her ticket away, the conductor moved over to Harvey's seat, but Harvey completely ignored him as he once again lit the cigarette he had placed back in his mouth. The conductor just leaned forward and smiled as he did with Kieli, and moved on to the next box of seats.

"Why didn't you show him your ticket?" Kieli complained on the conductor's behalf.

Harvey just glanced sideways at her and blew smoke diagonally up towards the ceiling. "Show who?"

"'Who?'" Kieli peered questioningly outside the box and cast her gaze at the conductor's back as he moved away from them down the aisle.

The seats were packed with travelers despite its being the middle of the Colonization Days vacation, but now that she looked, not one of them reacted to the appearance of the conductor as they carried on their own business — sleeping, chatting, etc. But the conductor went through the motions of looking carefully at each ticket, smiling kindly at each of them, and walking on.

After the uniformed back vanished through the door to the car in front of them, Kieli realized, a little late, that her ticket had already been checked yesterday, and by a different conductor. She let out a little "Ah!"

Of course the other passengers wouldn't have noticed him; he was a ghost in the shape of a conductor.

When she looked at Harvey, his hand was at his mouth holding his cigarette, as if to hide his smirk, and he was looking pointedly to the side. Kieli glared resentfully at him and said, "Tell me these things sooner!"

"Not my job."

". . . . . ." He didn't have to say it so flatly.

"He's not hurting anybody. He won't mind if you just leave him alone," the round speaker said in a calm voice; apparently the Corporal in the radio had realized long ago.

Somewhat embarrassed at being the only one who didn't figure it out right away, Kieli squirmed in her seat. She had mixed feelings about being in this odd situation. It was the exact opposite of all her previous circumstances, when she was the only one who could see spirits. But, thinking about it, she felt strangely relieved that the people who were with her could see the things she could see. She really was glad she had come with them. Although Harvey seemed to think she was a nuisance.

"I wonder what he's doing."

When Kieli expressed her simple curiosity over the spirit conductor's strange behavior, Harvey, in the opposite seat, had his eyes directed away from her as he puffed his cigarette and stated the obvious — "He's checking tickets" — in an unfriendly tone.

"I *wonder* what he's *doing*," she repeated more clearly than before, and cast her gaze firmly at her addressee's profile.

". . . Look." After she waited a full five seconds, her companion ran out of patience and a vein twitched in his temple. "Let's get one thing straight. This is advice from your elder. It's not like I'm telling you this because if you get involved with these troublesome ghosts and for some reason the sparks fly in my direction and threaten my peaceful schedule then that's a huge nuisance, but since that is the case, I'm telling you."

His cigarette hung from the corner of his mouth as he made his oddly worded introduction. He continued, "You let them take too much advantage of you. The reason people normally can't see them is that they're already dead and don't have that much influence in the world anymore, and they're not even little annoyances, so nobody can see them. If you want to live a normal life, then stop reacting every time you see one and just ignore it."

After taking a little time to digest the meaning of his long-winded speech, Kieli looked meekly down at her lap and thought that he might have a point. If she imagined she couldn't see anything, she should have been able to be like normal people. But that seemed like a very difficult task to Kieli.

"Augh, you don't have to look so sullen." Seeing Kieli so glumly deep in thought, Harvey ruffled his hair in exasperation and spat, with a bit of self-contempt, "I mean, it's not like I'm living a normal life myself."

That's when it happened.

The ghost conductor came back from the car ahead of them and passed through the aisle next to Kieli and the others again. Or rather, he ran through, kicking the hem of his uniform out of the way, with such incredible speed that it was as if a dark blue wind had blown by.

When Kieli poked her face into the aisle in surprise, he had already vanished through the door to the car behind them.

"I wonder what he's doing."

She tilted her head and returned to her original posture. Harvey was glaring at her with half-opened eyes. "I guess that troubled look on your face just now had nothing to do with my advice."

"It did, but this and that are . . ." Kieli was unable to finish her excuse. "Eh?"

Just then, the train was rocked by an abnormal centrifugal force, and the next thing she knew, Kieli's whole body was flung to the window. Her cheek pressed against the pane, and as her field of vision shook with the severe vibrations, the reddish-brown earth looked as if it was being pushed up toward her. Before her eyes, the window glass hit the ground and shattered, and Kieli frantically covered her head.

It all happened in an instant.

". . . eh?"

She opened her eyes very timidly, her arms still over her head.

The scenery had rotated ninety degrees. The flattened side wall was under her feet, and her soles rested on scattered pieces of glass. The ceiling was where the wall had been, and broken bulbs blinked with a listless, yellow light.

The passengers that had been flung out of their seats lay here and there in artless heaps, their limbs bent at odd angles, like dolls that had been tossed aside by an owner who had tired of them. A fine, blood-colored mist had settled toward the ground and was coiling around her ankles.

"Kieli."

It was just like that dream in the tunnel. A long, narrow, confined space; mountains of dead bodies as far as the eye could see.

"No . . ."

"Kieli, calm down."

Just as she was about to scream, someone grabbed her shoulders. "Don't get worked up. We're the only ones who can see this. The train is moving like normal," a low voice whispered in her ear. "Calm down," the voice admonished one more time, and she was brought back to reality.

She looked around her again, and nothing out of the ordinary had happened. The floor under her feet continued its regular vibrations, and the passengers were in their seats like before, passing the time by chatting, reading, or sleeping. Some of them looked dubiously at Kieli, who was standing with her arms over her head, but they didn't pay her much mind and quickly returned to their own business.

"Now sit."

Kieli felt a push at her shoulders and fell back into her seat with a thud. Harvey breathed a light sigh of relief and sat across from her.

She tried to ask him something, but her brain wasn't working very well, and her mouth flapped open and closed a few times before she finally managed a simple, "What was . . . ?" Harvey didn't say a word, just shoved his cigarette butt into the ashtray installed in the windowsill. The radio, sitting directly above the ashtray, answered instead. *"Probably the memories of the conductor's ghost. Must have died in the accident when the train turned sideways."*

"The conductor's . . ."

"But hey, for a normal human, you picked that up pretty vividly. You've got a rare condition. Hey Herbie, did you know there were people like this?"

"Picked up . . . ?"

Kieli turned a questioning gaze at Harvey, who made his usual correction of, "*Harvey,*" before sluggishly recrossing his legs where he sat and saying, "The moment a person dies, their strong emotions, regrets, and the like are released, right? Those memories are sewn over space and objects, and you end up picking up on them. It happens more easily when a spirit possessing those memories is close by."

"The memories of the dead . . ."

Kieli remembered the scene of the accident she saw a moment ago and stiffened. A bloody fog drifting through a closed space, piles of dead bodies. The conductor died in that terrible accident. Not only the conductor, but all the people riding the train, most likely including small children.

Before she knew it, the color had gone out of Kieli's hands. She clasped them tightly together.

"Don't let it bother you," Harvey said quietly, closing his eyes and sinking his tall figure into his seat as if planning to go to sleep. "He's already dead. It's not like you can do anything about it."

"If I can't do anything about it, why am I able to see it . . . ?" Kieli couldn't help saying. Harvey didn't answer.

Harvey and the radio both went silent after that, and Kieli, now with nothing to do, dozed a little, listening to a tune that was a more moderate tempo than the rock music from earlier.

The next thing she knew, she started to dream about the tunnel again. She thought, *It's that scary dream; I need to wake up*; but her body wouldn't move. In her heart she desperately implored, *Harvey, wake me up!* As soon as she did, she sensed someone next to her, and thanks to that person, she opened her eyes.

"Harve . . ." Relieved at having been pulled out of her nightmare, Kieli looked up to see the conductor in the dark blue uniform with gold buttons standing over her, peering at her. Out of reflex, Kieli started to get out her ticket, but then, realizing what she was doing, stopped her hand in her pocket.

Just like last time, the conductor nodded at her with his gentle smile as if to say, "You're okay." As expected, he did the same with Harvey (Harvey, of course, kept his eyes directed diagonally downward and ignored him, just like last time) and moved on to the next seat.

Kieli stood up from her seat a little and gaped at the conductor's back as he disappeared into the car ahead of them, performing the exact scene he had showed them earlier. When she sat back down, Harvey hadn't moved except to direct his half-opened eyes at her.

"Do you know what 'learning ability' is?"

"Don't you wonder what that conductor is doing?"

"No," Harvey said flatly, closing his eyes again. Kieli frowned, upset that he wouldn't pay any attention to her. Then, just like before, the conductor's spirit returned with a frantic look on his face. In the blink of an eye, he ran by Kieli and her fellow travelers and disappeared into the next car.

Not even a second later, the image of the accident assaulted Kieli once more. Kieli closed her eyes tight so she wouldn't see it, but the scene went on, ruthlessly realistic, on the other side of her eyelids. She was more calm than the first time, as she watched passengers being thrown around and crushed in the overturned train, but that calmness made her see the details all the more clearly.

She covered her head with her arms, and somehow managed to wait it out. "Harveyyyy . . ." She looked up, almost in tears, at Harvey, who sat up grudgingly and adjusted his position.

"You can look at me like that, but . . ."

At that moment, the same dark blue uniform stood next to the seat. Kieli started and looked up to see the exact same conductor with the exact same expression. The third time she saw it, his friendly smile started to look creepy. Even Harvey's jaw dropped a little, and he watched, weirded out, as the ghost in uniform left, his smile plastered to his face.

"Hey, what do you think he's doing?" This time, not even Harvey scoffed when Kieli asked the question for the umpteenth time — because he didn't have time. The conductor returned in less time than he did before, and immediately the disastrous vision of the car turning over spread before them. Before it vanished, the conductor came for the fourth time, walking through the dead and injured bodies on the ground, smiling and inspecting tickets. Kieli covered her mouth, feeling nauseated as she watched the convoluted scene.

"Don't you think something's strange? I thought he was a harmless spirit who had just fallen into an endless replay of his memories of the accident, but . . ." the radio said, a nervous air in his voice. "You're right," Harvey agreed, finally serious. *He didn't care a bit when I said it.* Kieli stood up, a little peeved.

"Kieli?" Harvey looked up at her, questioningly.

"I'm going after him," she answered shortly, and stepped into the aisle just as the conductor's spirit was about to disappear through the door to the deck between cars. She quickly chased after him.

"Herbie."

Behind her, she heard the radio shoo him out and sensed Harvey sighing and getting out of his seat.

The conductor's spirit passed over the uncovered deck and continued on to the next car. None of the passengers noticed the ghost walking down the aisle, and a sense of the weariness of traveling through the night accompanied the peaceful voices that drifted throughout the car.

Kieli went down the aisle at a trot and looked back once just in front of the door to the next car. Harvey wouldn't run but took long, very reluctant strides toward her, holding the radio in one hand.

Strangely, she felt a bit relieved seeing him. She turned back around and went out to the deck, where she was surprised to find the conductor's back halted immediately in front of her. The back suddenly turned around, and Kieli froze, her head almost ramming into his belly. Then she realized there was no way they would crash into each other. The conductor just went through Kieli's body and ran back the way he had come.

Kieli watched the conductor hurry off and looked back at the place he had been standing. It was in front of the couplers that linked the two cars. She held her hair back as the wind blew it every which way and looked down at her feet. The image of the track filled her view as it ran past, vibrating fiercely, and for a moment she felt dizzy.

Right in front of her shoes, the couplers, shaped like two large fists clenched together, rattled as the metal fittings struck each other. They collided with each other so violently that they jumped in time with the moving cars' vibrations.

She stood there, not grasping the meaning of the situation right away, when a voice came down from above her head.

"It's broken."

Kieli pointed her chin straight up and looked above her. Harvey was peering over her head at the couplers. He said it so matter-of-factly he might as well have said, "Toaster's broken. Guess I can't have toast this morning"; so for three more seconds, she still didn't take in the significance. After looking back down at the couplers, she finally realized that the fittings that held them in place were broken.

"Isn't that dangerous?"

"I dunno. If they're not careful, the train could derail."

Thinking, *And isn't that dangerous?*, Kieli looked incredulously back at Harvey and asked, "What should we do?" Harvey took on a thoughtful expression, like he was thinking something as trivial as, "Well, I can just have cereal instead of toast," and simply said, "If it starts to look really bad, I can just jump off, right?"

Kieli couldn't respond immediately; she gaped up at the face above her.

"*Why you . . . So you don't care as long as* you *can get away?*" the radio interjected in place of the speechless Kieli. Harvey blinked, apparently surprised that anyone was complaining, and looked down at the radio in his hand.

"No, I could carry you and Kieli."

"Never mind," Kieli said, not wanting to listen to this non-sense any longer, and she shoved aside the heartless giant who was blocking the door. She had to hurry and warn the conductor — the living conductor this time.

The instant she returned to the passenger car, the vision of the overturned car spread before her eyes. She froze for a second, but, realizing that the ghost conductor's memories were still on loop, she frantically shook the scene from her mind and ran down the aisle. The passengers in the real seats chatted peacefully, overlapping the illusion of the injured, looking up and sending dubious glances in her direction.

She kept going straight through the car she had been sitting in to the last car, finally catching up to the conductor's spirit.

The conductor stood still. Before his eyes lay his own dead body, part of his chest crushed in the accident. As he stared down at his corpse from his own memories, the conductor froze in terror.

The conductor hadn't made it. Most likely, he had discovered the broken couplers and run back to stop the train but didn't make in time and met his end here.

Kieli didn't stop; she ran past the conductor. The conductor may not have made it then, but Kieli could make it now — so that these tragic memories wouldn't become reality again.

"Mr. Conductor!" Kieli arrived at the conductor's room and slammed the door open. The *other* conductor, who had apparently been enjoying a leisurely breakfast, looked up in surprise.

"It's terrible! The couplers are loose! That car back there!" In broken sentences, Kieli, out of breath, frantically tried to explain the situation. The conductor, a sandwich stuffed in his mouth, wore a blank expression and said something like "Wha ha maher?" Kieli nearly exploded with frustration and waved her arms violently up and down.

"I *said* the couplers are broken! Hurry and stop the train!"

Perhaps her fearsome rage overwhelmed him, because the conductor picked up the intercom that connected to the engine room. He gulped down his sandwich, pounded his chest, and cleared his throat, then turned to the mouthpiece and drawled, "Uhh . . ." Kieli couldn't wait any longer; she snatched the transmitter from the conductor.

"Slow down immediately! There's going to be a big accident!" she barked curtly and shoved the phone back at the stunned conductor. She flew out of the conductor's room with the same force with which she had run in, and dashed back toward the front car, shouting, "We're making an emergency stop! Grab onto something!" to the passengers on either side of her.

Harvey, gazing at the train tracks, realized that they had put on the brakes. At the same time, he also realized that they probably wouldn't stop in time. The front cars were approaching a gentle right-hand curve.

"Herbie!" the radio urged from his hand.

"Harvey," Harvey sighed briefly. "I'm not really a friend of the people, serving the public for no compensation. For that matter, I'd actually prefer mankind be destroyed. Every night, I pray to the heavens that an asteroid will hit the planet, but my wish never comes true."

"Kieli does everything she can. I like that." The radio's answer didn't really connect; apparently he didn't want to talk about the destruction of mankind.

"What, you're getting attached? Didn't you want to go back to your grave?" Harvey asked maliciously, a smirk rising to his lips. The radio stayed silent.

Heaving another sigh, Harvey reluctantly started to tie the radio's cord to the deck's handrail. *If I hadn't gotten mixed up with that girl, I wouldn't have to go to all this trouble.* He didn't want to take anyone with him in the first place, and if the Church found him out, it would be trouble. Now that he thought of it, he did have the option of shutting her up permanently — but of course at this point in the journey, he didn't feel inclined to do that.

"Gah, what the hell am I doing . . . ?" he moaned. When he finished tying the radio to the rail, a strong centrifugal force pulled him to the left. The rattling sound from the joined couplers came to an abrupt stop and the car opposite him floated upward.

"Damn it, my arm *just* healed," he grumbled to no one in particular as he took the rail with his right hand, planted himself firmly on the deck, and reached for the couplers with his free hand. He grabbed the coupler from the other car and forced it back to the one in front of him, and held them together with the full weight of his body. "Stupid! Just go back . . . !" The intense shaking traveled through his arm and rattled his brain. As he put the couplers together, they caught the skin of his fingers and tore the flesh off. He lost concentration for just a second when he felt a sharp pain run through him, like his fingers were being twisted off, but he soon gathered his wits and shook off the pain, leaving only a faint, unpleasant throbbing sensation in the core of his brain.

Suddenly, the brakes kicked in, and the radio hanging from the handrail swung violently. When he caught sight of the radio's cord coming undone and the radio flying into the air, Harvey involuntarily let go of the handrail and grabbed the cord.

"Ah . . ." *Damn,* he thought, as he and the radio slid sideways and were thrown off the deck. *"Herbie, you idio —"* the radio's jeers were lost in the high-pitched screech of metal scraping metal.

"Harvey!" He faintly heard a girl's voice through the ear-shattering din and stopped breathing as, without warning, something squeezed his neck from behind. Kieli had jumped through the car door and was clinging to the hem of his jacket. She strangled him with such force that any normal person would surely have suffocated as she pulled him back toward her, and he fell to the deck, taking the small girl with him.

It looked as if time had stopped temporarily as one of the cars remained suspended in the air and then thudded back onto the track.

The train had stopped.

The screech of the brakes, the shaking of the cars, the howl of the wind — all sound stopped abruptly, and a terrible quiet fell over their surroundings. After a few seconds of silence, the murmuring of the passengers — some anxious, some relieved — finally reached their ears.

". . . What the hell am I doing . . . ?"

Still lying faceup on the deck, Harvey let out all the breath he had been holding, just as his exhaustion overcame him. "Harvey, you're heavy." Kieli struggled under the arm he had flung to the side, but he was tired and chose not to move it for a while.

Kieli was told that they wanted to send her a letter of thanks, but since this was of course the first time in Kieli's life that she had had such an experience — and on top of that, she was not used to receiving so much praise — her first reaction was to politely decline.

"And how can we ever thank you, sir?" The conductor (the one who was eating a sandwich) took off his hat and bowed deeply to Harvey. "I'll call the rescue party right away. We have to get you patched up."

Harvey acted indifferent to the thanks paid him and Kieli, but when he heard the second part, he yelped in panic. "No, that won't be necessary. And I don't want your thanks, either. If you have men with enough time to waste writing thank-you notes, why don't you put them on the maintenance team?" Kieli couldn't tell if Harvey's refusal was polite or rude, but he dragged her off, just as she was starting to think it might not be so bad to get a thank-you letter, and ran away from the conductor.

The long, gray train stood on the wilderness tracks like a dead snake. Railroad company emergency cars from the east and west sandwiched the train, and the company was about to start investigating the accident.

The passengers had been forced to disembark and stood in circles near the track, complaining about the accident and confirming each other's safety. Kieli heard, from fragments of their conversations, that a similar train accident had happened in the past. Apparently a pair of couplers had been broken, and every car behind the break had derailed; many people had been killed or injured. One of the victims had been the train's conductor.

Kieli was in danger of falling as Harvey dragged her along with his left hand, his stride easily twice the length of her own. She noticed that his hand was covered in blood.

"Harvey, are you okay?"

"Why?" Harvey slowed down a bit and turned around. After

following Kieli's gaze, he looked as if he was only just noticing it himself. He said, "Oh, sorry. I got your coat dirty," and let go.

"I don't care about that. Let me see it." Kieli took his blood-covered hand back in hers and pulled it toward herself. The skin from his fingertips to his palm was stripped off, and it was bright red with fresh blood.

She started to look away from the awful state of his hand, but when she looked closer, she saw that the bleeding had mostly stopped. Instead, the blackish liquid, like coal tar, was oozing out and starting to coil around the wound the way it did when his neck got hurt at the old station.

"That can't be fun to watch," Harvey said gruffly in response to her stares. He pulled his hand away and shoved it into his coat pocket.

"Doesn't it hurt?"

"Eh, I can ignore it. I've been trained that way."

Harvey had quickened his pace again, and he soon left Kieli behind. She hurried after him and looked over Harvey's shoulder at his profile. Kieli didn't know what it was like to be able to ignore pain, but she figured that didn't equal *not* hurting. While she thought about it, Harvey went back to the bags they had left by the side of the track and, his left hand still in his pocket, used his other hand to pick up his backpack and the radio.

"We're walking to the next station. Is that okay with you?"

Kieli stopped for a moment and whined in protest. She had heard that the emergency cars would be taking groups of passengers to the next station.

"I don't want them asking annoying questions. It's not that far."

Kieli doubted whether or not something that "wasn't that far" for Harvey's long gait would be "not that far" for her, but

Harvey showed no interest in hearing her opinion and started walking. Feeling that if she sulked too much, he would say something like, "If you don't like it, you can ride the train by yourself," Kieli sped up and followed him.

As soon as she started walking, she felt someone watching her from behind and turned around to see the conductor's spirit standing in the distance. Still wearing his kind smile, he stayed beside the train as if protecting it.

The conductor removed his hat and bowed deeply in thanks. She felt as though she could hear a voice say, "Thank you." Under her breath, Kieli murmured a good-bye.

"Kieli. If your legs are too short, I'll carry you."

"I'm coming. Wait up." Kieli didn't really understand what Harvey had said, but his words urged her on, and she trotted up to him. They started walking on the track, side by side.

The train track continued in a straight line through the wilderness to the horizon hung with sand-colored gas. Far in the distance, she could just make out the next town.

CHAPTER 3

CHEERS FOR THE BLOOD-COVERED CLOWN

As night approached, people filled the main street, literally to overflowing, and no one knew how in the world the town could accommodate them. Instruments played in cacophony, and decorative lights with practically no sense of unity painted a scene of festive excitement that spread throughout.

Night shops selling toys and junk food lined the streets; passersby were called with shouts to see the shows at booths; cheers and jeers were given to roadside magicians and fire-ring jugglers; musical troupes paraded by as each member played his own melody on his instrument — it was as if someone had turned a toy box upside down and then jumbled everything up even more. Seeing it, Kieli forgot the exhaustion of the day and spent a while staring in amazement.

As expected, Harvey's definition of "not that far" was completely unreliable, and they had walked at least half the day since the train accident that morning. They finally arrived at the station close to evening. They checked when the next train would be leaving. Harvey and Kieli went into town a little before sunset.

It was a run-down country town; the cold wind from Easterbury's eastern wilderness blew through the litter-strewn streets. They walked for a while along the quiet main street and found a cheap hotel. The unfriendly man at the front desk took his time checking them in, and they had to wait thirty minutes before he produced a key from behind the reception desk. By the time they made it into their room, night had fallen completely.

Kieli slowly dragged her leaden feet onto her bed, but just as she figured the town seemed pretty boring and she might as well go to sleep, the streets under her window appeared to hold a different world than they did half an hour ago.

Apparently, during the Colonization Days holidays, lots of

peddlers and entertainment troupes gathered in this town to hold a carnival every night.

Kieli sat on her pillow with her chin on one knee, looking out her window at the streets below. "Let's go take a little look. Since we're staying here tonight anyway," she said, looking back at the room. Because of the accident, the train that was supposed to be leaving that night wouldn't be running, and the trains weren't going to start up again until the next morning. Even the passengers who had taken the emergency cars and arrived in town one step ahead of them were stuck there until the next day.

But, in contrast to Kieli's high spirits, a weary voice leaked out of the radio sitting on the side table: *"Give me a break. I'll pass. There are too many loud, showy thoughts in this town. It makes my eyes spin."*

"Old men don't do so well in showy places," Harvey added, lying on the bed on the other side of the table. He pulled a box of cigarettes out of his pocket, caring neither about the radio's retort of *"You're one to talk about people's ages,"* nor the rusty plate on the side table that read "no smoking in bed" and looked like it had already been burned.

Before Kieli could even ask, "You're going, aren't you, Harvey?" he shot her down with "I'm passing, too. It's too much trouble, and I don't care." Kieli felt like the only one rising above the room's weary atmosphere, and after a few moments of silence, she muttered, "Fine. Then I'll go by myself."

She sat on the edge of her bed and began to put her shoes back on. They were black leather boots that matched her uniform, and while she took time to tie up the laces, Harvey, who had gotten into bed with his shoes still on, breathed a sigh and got up.

Kieli looked blankly up at him, still bent over.

"I'll go with you as far as the front door. I'm out of ciga-rettes," Harvey said, throwing his empty, crumpled cigarette box into the wastebasket and reaching for his coat. Kieli hur-ried as fast as she could to tie her shoes.

When they set foot outside of the hotel entrance, they were smack in the middle of the festivities on the main street. The temperature had gone down with the sun, but once Kieli entered the crowds, the cold no longer bothered her, and wrapped in the heat from those around her, she was actually quite warm.

A mass of people had formed on the shoulder of the road right next to her. A gentlemanly looking peddler wearing a tall chapeau and bowtie was standing in the center of the ring of people, selling something. Kieli's interest was piqued; she poked her head between the tall adults and peeked in at his booth.

The man in the chapeau was selling something that appeared to be a small, cubic box. There was a peephole in one side, and as people held the boxes and looked inside, they sighed in ad-miration, laughed, and sometimes screamed. She watched for a while, wondering what it was, and eventually the peddler noticed her, beckoned her over, and offered her a box.

Tilting her head in curiosity, Kieli followed the example of the others and put one eye up to the peephole.

"Wow . . ." She let out a noise in spite of herself.

The box held a world inside it. Every time she changed the angle, the images through the peephole changed one after an-other, projecting all kinds of scenes. Each one was a world from somewhere on the planet that Kieli had only seen in books. The mechanized Church Capital, the ruins said to have once been a spaceship, a ship that crosses the Sand Ocean. . . . Surprising her even further, the images inside the box moved, and a sandworm, like a giant snake monster, dug a tunnel, following after the ship as it ran across the sand at full speed.

The sandworm suddenly turned around to face her, and, opening its empty, elliptical mouth wide, it came flying at the peephole, as if to swallow Kieli's eyeball.

"Eeeeek!"

Kieli flung the box away in surprise. "Oof." If Harvey hadn't caught her from behind, Kieli would have landed on her rear in the crowd.

The man in the chapeau caught the box, smiling in satisfaction. Apparently he enjoyed seeing people's startled reactions. His poor taste annoyed Kieli, but she soon let out a small laugh. The peddler's boxes pleased the customers, and the customers' reactions pleased the peddler. At this carnival, ordinary people, peddlers, and entertainers alike all made up the audience, and all played the clown.

Still, she didn't have to let it scare her so much that she fell over. She snickered, half shocked at herself, and a cool voice fell from above her head: "Was it that much fun?"

"Why don't you try it, Harvey? It's really fun," Kieli suggested, looking up at Harvey and feeling a bit mischievous at the thought of how nice it would be if the box surprised Harvey.

"He's just fooling bumpkins. In Westerbury, 3-D projections aren't anything special," Harvey uttered with every bit of disinterest, as he opened his new box of cigarettes. It seemed Harvey had no intention of being an audience member or a clown.

"You're no fun. So you knew?" Kieli pouted, discouraged. "So you've been to Westerbury, Harvey?"

". . . I've *stayed* in Westerbury," he said with a subtle correction.

Kieli remembered the stories Becca had told her about the images projected on the walls of the buildings in Westerbury. In Westerbury, they probably projected huge three-dimensional images on screens tens, hundreds of times bigger than those boxes, and multicolored lights decorated the streets. When she heard about it from Becca, it seemed to have so little to do with her that she couldn't even imagine it, but now she could wrap her mind around the idea of that scenery, at least better than she could before.

"I'm going back after we've gone around once," Harvey said, setting out into the hustle and bustle. Following after him at a trot as he zigzagged his way through (he said he was just going to buy cigarettes, but evidently he felt like sticking around for a while), Kieli looked up over his shoulder at his profile with more than a little envy. It was possible that Harvey had been to the mechanized capital and the Sand Ocean. Maybe he even crossed the continent on a ship over the sand, and visited the ruins of the spaceship.

The Corporal had said that Harvey wandered all over the planet in the eighty years since the War ended. To Kieli, eighty years was such a long time, it might as well be eternity. She wondered if he traveled alone all that time before he picked up the Corporal.

A troupe of musicians in red-and-green-striped breeches and yellow tights passed by, playing haphazard melodies at high volumes, derailing Kieli's train of thought. Kieli covered her ears with both hands, but smiled as she shouted, "That's so weird!" and watched them go. On the other side of the street, some large, half-naked, red-faced men were twisting iron pipes, as spectators waved their fists in the air and excitedly made bets over who could touch the opposite ends together fastest.

Moving on, Kieli came near a skinny man who was trying to

swallow a sword that was about as long as she was tall. When she saw it, she let out a little cry.

"Harvey, Harvey, that man's going to die!"

Without thinking, Kieli ran forward a few steps and pointed. As she did so, she looked back to see Harvey with an expression more of consternation than interest. He asked, as he did before, "Is it that much fun?"

Kieli stopped and stared at him, still pointing.

Now that he mentioned it, it was true — she had been acting strangely cheerful for a while, bouncing around and making a lot of noise all by herself. Even she couldn't tell what she was so merry about.

When she lowered her arm, puzzling over her own behavior, someone wearing a white glove offered a hand to her from behind. The hand came out of a sleeve wearing fluttery fringe and held the string of an orange balloon. When she turned around, more balloons of varying colors surrounded her, and there stood a clown whose face was painted white with blue stars.

"Th-thank you . . ." Kieli blinked two or three times and tried to accept the balloon but immediately let out a short gasp.

The clown was covered in blood. A thin line of it formed a circle around his neck, and it poured down from his decorative collar and all its ruffles, dying his white clown costume red. Half of the paint on his face had come off, too, and only the blue stars around his eyes and the rouge that formed a smile on his mouth managed to remain.

As Kieli stood speechless, the clown, a smile still stuck on his face, held out the balloon once more. Kieli impulsively withdrew her hand and shrunk back, looking to Harvey for help.

"Ha —"

"Harvey!"

It wasn't Kieli who called out first. But the Corporal never called him Harvey; so as far as Kieli knew, she should have been the only one who would say that name.

"Harvey!" the high voice called again, carrying surprisingly well through the tumult, and then a hand reached over from the side and pulled on the sleeve of Harvey's coat. Perhaps it had taken Harvey by surprise, because he stumbled a step and turned around, gaping. A woman pulled herself out of the crowd and jumped in front of him.

"It *is* you! Wow, you haven't changed a bit! I knew it was you the minute I saw you! I didn't think I'd see you in this town. Could it be you came here to see me? Oh no, what do I do? I don't want to be unfaithful, but . . . !" the woman started chattering away, connecting one sentence to another with an energy that even the crowd's enthusiasm couldn't outdo. On the other hand, Harvey, not quite able to grasp the situation, did not hesitate to say, "Umm, who are you again?" But after looking down at the woman's face for a second, he seemed to remember, let out an, "Aaahh!" then opened and closed his mouth a few times.

"Don't 'Aaahh' me. You didn't recognize me? Ugh, that part of you hasn't changed, either." The woman stuck out her painted lips in a pout. But her smile returned in no time. She wrapped her arms around one of Harvey's and said, "You have time to talk, right? I just got on my break! I want to surprise the troupe leader. You really haven't changed at all!"

"No, sorry, but . . ." Harvey tried to decline at first. ". . . So Shiman's here?" he murmured, a thoughtful look on his face. He glanced in Kieli's direction.

Kieli was standing a few steps away from them, her mouth still open from when she started to call Harvey's name. The clown, despite holding so many very conspicuous balloons, had disappeared completely.

"Kieli, I'm going to go talk for a bit. What do you want to do? You can come if you want."

"You're with someone?"

Apparently that was the first time the woman noticed Kieli. She stared wide-eyed in her direction, so Kieli closed her mouth and stared back. Her bouncy, high voice sounded like it could be a teenage girl's, but she looked a few years older than Harvey, as if she was in her early twenties. Judging by her bright makeup and the sparkling light blue costume that covered her body in feathers from head to toe, she might have been a singer or a dancer or something. But her limbs and face were relatively plump; she was the type of woman one might call "cute."

After wondering suspiciously who the woman might be, the obvious thought finally occurred to Kieli that, regardless of Harvey's antisocial personality, he had traveled for a long time, so it wouldn't be too strange for him to have acquaintances. From Harvey's perspective, the few days that Kieli had known him must've felt no longer than the blink of an eye.

"What? What's the deal with the girl!? Don't tell me you just didn't know what to do and got involved in something criminal!"

"Who didn't know what to do about what? Don't shout that stuff; you'll give people the wrong idea. . . . She just started tagging along after me on her own," Harvey responded to the high-pitched, fast-talking voice with a grim expression. He might not have been trying to imply anything, and it *was* actually the case, but the words still stung Kieli. She suddenly felt as if Harvey had placed some distance between them, and her high spirits of a moment ago came crashing down.

"I'm fine. I'm going to look around a little more."

The tumult swallowed her mumbles, and they may not have reached him, but she turned and started to walk away. "Kieli!

Hey!" She stopped, feeling like his act of calling her back had saved her somewhat, but Harvey only added, "Go on back without me. I'll be back by morning at the latest."

Some passersby got between them, and it wasn't until after she had started walking, the tide of people carrying her along, that Kieli realized the meaning of those words. . . . Back by morning!

Just once, when she was very small, her grandmother had taken her to a carnival like this. Thinking about it now, she realized that her grandmother's aged hand, the hand that held Kieli's so tightly as she was jostled around between the legs of so many adults, couldn't have had much strength in it, but the warmth that connected them promised little Kieli the highest degree of protection and security.

Those hands had gone long ago to a place where Kieli could no longer touch them, and now Kieli walked alone as the waves of carnivalgoers pushed against her.

Ignoring manners, she popped a stick of yellow candy in her mouth (even one stick of candy would seem like a waste to the normal Kieli's financial sense; but today, when she saw it at a booth, she felt like buying it) and walked with her face down and both hands in her coat pockets. The musical troupe she passed by earlier now caught up with her from behind.

The trumpeter blasted a broken *brr-rrrm* in Kieli's face; the flute player danced around her, and finally, a sudden gust from the cymbals crashing right before her eyes blew her bangs up, and the musical troupe went on its way. Kieli watched them and saw that they wound their way around other passersby in the same manner and basically teased the pedestrians as they paraded on, playing their individual parts however they pleased, but the people they harassed looked very pleased as they covered their ears.

Kieli was the only one to see them off with a blank expression as she sucked on her candy. The current Kieli was neither an audience member nor a clown.

Now that she was alone like this, she thought it was very strange that she had been in such high spirits until a short while ago. At the boarding school, if anything, she was a very sober person.

Somehow I'm different than usual. I guess it's been since I met Harvey and the Corporal . . . she thought, vaguely. Her feet moved naturally away from the main street, as if avoiding busy places. When she left the heat of the crowd, the cold of the night that she had once forgotten seeped in through her coat, and, thanks to it, her stuffy feelings cleared up a bit.

She wandered into an alley beside a circus tent and came out to a vacant lot where she discovered the blood-covered clown again. The white clown costume appeared to be floating in the gloom of the lot.

The clown was practicing juggling knives. He started with two and juggled with light, rhythmic motions. While they were in the air, he would add a knife with one hand. Three knives, four, five — when he missed, he started from the beginning.

Just as the Corporal said back at the hotel, the excited thoughts of a large number of people jumble together at carnivals, and it was like those feelings had erased Kieli's ability to sense spirits. In this quiet place, where the tumult of the main street was only so much noise, she could tell right away.

No matter how much he practiced, he would never be able to show anyone. Kieli stopped and watched for a while as the clown's ghost focused all his attention on his practice.

He threw the knife with one hand and caught it with the other; now he threw it higher, passed his hand under his leg, and . . . missed. The illusion knife grazed the clown's hand and stabbed the ground with a *thunk*. The clown raised a foot and jumped back in girlish surprise. It was so funny, Kieli couldn't help laughing.

The clown stopped and looked back at her. Even with the paint peeling pitifully off his face, he opened his mouth and gave Kieli his very best clown smile.

In a bar, one street over from the carnival's main thorough-fare, gathered a motley group of peddlers, street performers on break, and sightseers who had grown tired of playing out-side and had come in to get warm. None of them seemed to have anything in common, but they mingled together. They filled a hall wrapped in dim lights and the smell of alcohol with a flurry of multicultural excitement.

"Huh. The abandoned mine, eh?" a middle-aged man said thoughtfully from the other side of the round table, lighting his umpteenth cigarette with his favorite silver lighter.

"You been there, Shiman?"

"Nobody's got any business in that place. There's nothing but graves. Haven't *you* been there? I thought you'd been everywhere on the planet."

"My feet just never took me to Easterbury," Harvey said, smiling wryly as he took advantage of the flame to light his own cigarette.

The man closed his eyes and muttered, "Right. That was the field of your last battle, wasn't it . . . ?"

Shiman was one of the rare people who had a lasting friend-ship with Harvey and was one of the few Harvey trusted with his true identity. He was the leader of a troupe of dancers and street performers who toured all over, and, as they both did a lot of traveling, sometimes they would run into each other like this. Come to think of it, he could easily have guessed that they would be visiting this town during carnival season.

On the other side of the narrow wisp of smoke that rose from the end of the cigarette in his mouth, Harvey looked at his old friend's face with mixed emotions. They had met twenty or thirty years ago; at the time, he was nothing more than an acrobat, but now he had the full dignity of a troupe leader, and, while it was only natural, Harvey found that the wrinkles in his face deepened proportionally every time they met.

Just then, cheers erupted in the middle of the hall, and he turned his head to see a very cheerful, very drunk street performer with a fat belly begin to demonstrate his fire-breathing abilities to the surrounding guests. There was a scuffle with the barkeep, who interjected, shouting at him to take it outside so as not to start a fire, and jeers flew from the other tables to agitate the situation.

"He with you?"

"He's all brawn and no brain," Shiman chuckled, nodding. Apparently this was a familiar scene, and he made no effort to mediate.

"Have any of your clowns ever died?" Harvey asked, remembering suddenly as he watched the excitement in the hall, his head resting on his hand. The look on Shiman's face asked, "What's this all of a sudden?" His cigarette hand stopped on its way to his mouth, and he frowned as if recalling something not particularly pleasant.

"It wasn't one of our clowns, but there was an incident about this time ten years ago, where an inspecting party came to this town from the capital. A bigwig from the Church thought that a clown was mocking him with his performance and had him beheaded. Since then, there haven't been any clowns in this town."

"I see . . ."

"What's this about clowns?" a bright voice interjected. Harvey stopped his pondering and looked up, dodging the question with a vague smile. "Oh, nothing."

The woman he had met outside stood holding a glass of diluted whiskey in each hand. She exchanged one of them for Shiman's now-empty one, then, catching sight of Harvey's glass, she asked, mystified, "Oh, you're not drinking?"

Her question made Harvey realize for the first time that he had forgotten to touch his drink. Thanks to his seemingly fortunate condition of having an internal power source that removed the need to take in external nourishment, if he wasn't careful, basic human actions like eating and drinking slipped his mind. Although his rebellious nature did foster his persistent habit of smoking.

"Just leave it there, Augusta." Shiman came to his rescue, waving his hand to shoo her away. "Go over there. The air's bad here."

"It would be fine if you didn't smoke." Augusta pouted, but relented unexpectedly easily and went away, leaving the glass on the table. Harvey thought something was strange as he watched her walk toward the brawl with the fire breather at its center.

"She's carrying a baby. This is her last carnival before she retires from dancing," Shiman explained, exhaling smoke without a qualm.

Harvey looked back at Shiman and blinked, then returned his gaze to the woman, who had gotten rather plump for a star dancer, and nodded in consent. Now that he thought of it, she would be old enough for that by now. When he last chanced on Shiman and his troupe, Augusta had been in the troupe for only a year and was about seventeen or eighteen. As a matter of fact, when she first called to him, he remembered her face but couldn't recall her name — it was no wonder, since a girl he thought was younger than him was suddenly an adult woman, passing him in age.

Augusta had gotten between the barkeep and the fire-breather, stopping the scuffle, and was looking straight at the fire-breathing man, unafraid despite his being twice her size, and saying something in a stern tone of voice. The fire-breather shrunk back, dejected, as she scolded him, and Harvey watched, impressed.

"That's her husband?" Harvey wasn't asking so much as confirming something he had noticed, but out of the corner of his eye, he saw Shiman nod in the affirmative.

"He's stupid, but honest. He'll make her happy. Five years ago, she was obsessed with you, but she's completely settled down now."

"Ha, ha . . ." he let out a dry laugh, and, as he was already trying to avoid the subject, he lit a new cigarette. So it had already been five years. Of course Augusta would be surprised that he hadn't changed; he'd better not see her again. Five years was the time period he had sort of decided on as the limit at which point he would cut off relations with people.

Augusta was barking out orders — the fire-breather would of course pay for damages, and she made the customers who participated in the ruckus help clean up the fallen tables and dishes that lay scattered around the floor.

"So what's this about a girl you have with you? What brought that about? If she has no relatives and needs a place to go, then we can take her in. . . ."

As the noise in the hall went down a notch, Shiman changed the subject. He probably made the offer because he knew that Harvey preferred not to be involved with other people too much. Grateful for his friend's consideration, he shook his head lightly. "She has a place to go. I'll send her back next week. Besides, I'm surprised at how interesting it is to watch her. Actually, I'm kind of enjoying it," he said, breathing out his honest feelings along with a puff of smoke.

Something about Kieli seemed to prevent her from getting too close to normal people, and he thought she might be surprisingly like himself. On the other hand, she would react so sensitively to beings that weren't normal humans — like that girl who called herself her roommate or whatever, and that conductor from this morning — that it was almost disgusting. Then, when he realized that, she would suddenly start acting like a normal girl after all, getting excited at all those old carnival acts.

He honestly never thought he would encounter anything that would seem so new to him at this point in his life. He had seen every single thing the planet had to offer and was quite sick of it all.

"Well, it's about time I got going," he said, for some reason. He smothered his still-fresh cigarette in the ashtray.

"Oh." Shiman smiled sadly, a bit disappointed, and raised his glass in farewell. "Let's meet again. We're planning to leave the East when the Colonization Days are over."

"Yeah. I'm glad we could talk," he answered with a smile, getting up from his chair. Apparently Augusta had gotten to a good stopping place; she left the cleanup to the men and ran up to Harvey.

"Harvey, don't tell me you're leaving? Let's talk all night!"

"You're pregnant, Augusta," Shiman interjected, exasperated. She retorted, "Oh, I can stay up *one* night!" looking indifferent (she was about the only one who could talk to the troupe leader as an equal), and, turning to Harvey for support, added, "You can stay, right?" Harvey smiled bitterly and shook his head.

"I'm leaving. My princess must be missing me. I'll come see you again after you have the baby." He wasn't used to refusing so diplomatically, and as he pacified her, he inwardly hoped that she couldn't tell he was lying — he had just decided that he would try not to run into them again. Part of it was that he knew he wouldn't get off with just a "You haven't changed!" if he met Augusta again, but more than anything, it was getting harder and harder to see Shiman's face. He might be an old man the next time they met. *I wish I could get a break already. I just don't want to watch people grow old anymore. . . .*

The ghost clown's slender fingers moved nimbly, twisting the balloons in knots; he created one round balloon animal after another and released them into the blue-gray night sky. A droopy-eared dog, a hook-tailed cat, a flock of yellow pigeons, a sand lion, even the sheep and guinea fowl normally used for food. The ship that came to colonize brought only a few types of animals, so there wasn't much variety on this planet; it was possible that the clown had learned how to make every animal in the encyclopedia.

After that, he did some hat tricks and balanced on a ball, performed a funny little silent one-man comedy act, and showed her the knife juggling he had been practicing earlier. This time, he succeeded in catching the knife under his leg, and, from Kieli's place on the empty lot's bench, she cried out, "You did it! Amazing, amazing!" She showered him with praise and cheers with all her heart.

Before she knew it, the balloon animals had gathered on

the bench to her right and left, imitating Kieli and clapping their hands. Kieli burst out laughing and kept applauding with the animals.

Time passed, and when the clown removed his hat and took a bow to signal the end of his final act, tears were running down Kieli's cheeks.

" . . . . . "

When she stopped clapping, the animals stopped with her. The lot instantly fell quiet, and the faint din from the main street started to sound louder. In reality, only Kieli's voice and applause had existed in the empty lot to begin with.

"Sorry, sorry. I'm okay . . ." While the clown and balloon animals watched over her, unsure what to do, Kieli wiped her tears with her coat sleeve and laughed it off.

She remembered when she was little and had sat next to her grandmother, clapping with all her might. She got the feeling that that carefree, happy little girl had disappeared somewhere when her grandmother died, and since then, she naturally stopped opening her heart much to people. Becca was the one friend she ever had; but she, too, had gone where she belonged, and now she, like her grandmother, was in a place Kieli could not reach. She had met Harvey and the ghost in the radio in Becca's place, but, of course, they weren't normal living people, either.

Now that she thought of it, Kieli only felt comfortable when she was with dead people.

Maybe I just haven't realized, and I've been a ghost all this time, too. . . . It was impossible to tell if the thought was joking or serious; as soon as it occurred to her, a balloon dog that had been peering at her, worried, perked its ears, burst, and disappeared with a little pop. The other animals followed, bursting one after another like bubbles. Kieli sensed someone's presence and raised her face.

Turning around, she saw a tall, redheaded man standing behind the bench.

"Hey, you. Why weren't you back in the room? I've been looking for you. What are you fooling around here for?" Harvey said in a light tone, leaning over her to look into her face. His jaw dropped, and then, "Huh? What? Why are you crying?"

"Shut up. Weren't you gonna come back in the morning?" She was deliberately short with him as she hurried to wipe her face.

Her reply took Harvey completely by surprise, and he blinked. "Is *that* what you're crying about?"

"No," Kieli retorted, looking down, suddenly angry, and stood up from the bench. *He doesn't understand people's concerns.*

"Sorry, sorry. I finished my business," Harvey said, ruffling Kieli's hair with one hand. "Stop it!" Kieli cried, and tried to brush him away, but he caught her hand easily.

"Let's go back. The Corporal's gotten bored and is doing nothing but whining. After he's the one that said he'd stay in the hotel by himself, the old fogey," he said as if nothing was the matter, keeping her hand in his as he started to walk off.

Kieli sulked but let him pull her by the hand. After she had gone a few steps, she stopped and turned around to see the clown's ghost, standing alone in the middle of the empty lot, waving his white hands. The balloon animals had returned and floated around the clown, and they all waved together.

Kieli smiled, too, and gave a small wave with her free hand. Beside her, Harvey smiled wryly and tugged lightly at her hand.

"Let's go."

Turning away from the clown and his company, the two headed back.

The injury from the train accident this morning still inflamed the hand that held hers. His large palm and long, rough fingers wrapped themselves around Kieli's hand that had nearly frozen over, now that she stopped to notice it. It was completely different from the wrinkly hand of her grandmother that lingered in her memory; it was a strange sensation, touching this hand for the first time. But Kieli felt the same comforting warmth from his palm that she had felt then, and she returned the grasp, not wanting to let it go.

CHAPTER 4

"I'M HOME."

Kieli could feel the cold of the concrete against her back through her coat. She shivered and pulled the collar of her coat closed, looking up at the rusty orange sky through an opening in the alley.

Tonight would be another cold one. Once the Colonization Days vacation ended, it would already be winter.

Still, the school-designated coat suited this situation very well, Kieli thought in a bit of self-derision as she considered her black clothes and her current position. Now if only she put on a pair of sunglasses, it would be perfect. She remembered a children's detective novel that she had borrowed from the library in her boredom during the previous year's Colonization Days, which only increased her boredom (and real detectives probably didn't wear such obvious clothing).

"Corporal, can't we go back now? It's bad taste to follow people around," she suggested for the umpteenth time, looking up at the sky as she plastered herself against the wall, but the small radio hanging from the cord around her neck replied with the villainous line, *"Shut up and follow him,"* immediately dismissing the idea.

Kieli sighed in exasperation but nevertheless did as she was told and peered stealthily into the opposite street from the shadows of the alley. Some way off, she could see the back of a tall man walking the rather empty old streets. The twilight sky dyed his copper-colored hair an even rustier dark orange.

His back looked as if it would turn this way for a second, and, *"Wah! He'll spot us. Hide!"* she drew her head back, as if pulled by the radio's voice.

She waited a while, her heart pounding, then moved her head to look one more time as Harvey veered onto a side street a little ways ahead.

"He's turning. Hurry!" the radio urged, swinging at the end of its cord.

". . . It's bad taste to follow people around," Kieli said, justifying herself with a grumble, as she ran out into the alley and went after the vanishing back at a trot.

How did I end up playing detective in the first place?

They stayed one night in the town with the carnival, then boarded the train that had started running again that morning, and arrived at their destination a little before dusk. It was a big transfer station on the eastern outskirts of the Easterbury parish, where the railroads met from all four directions. They had come from the central region of western Easterbury. If they kept going east, they would reach the Sand Ocean in the far east; if they went north, they would pass into the Northhairo parish, where the Church Capital and the mechanized capital were.

The last railroad, to the south, had been abolished and was no longer in use, but the abandoned mines that Kieli and Harvey headed for lay at the end of that deserted track. Harvey said it wasn't that far, so she figured it was quite far, and sure enough, it would take them from morning to night to walk the distance; Kieli whined, and they scheduled their departure for the next morning.

And so they found an inn near the station where they could stay the night, at which point Harvey said there was a place he wanted to stop by, and he'd set out on his own.

"It bothers me, that heartless bastard having a place he'd go to the trouble of visiting," the radio said, feigning all seriousness, and ordered Kieli to follow him. She grumbled — again — that it was bad taste to follow people, but in the end, Kieli did as she was told. Because it wasn't as if she wasn't secretly curious herself.

She stopped for a moment at the corner of the alley Harvey had gone down and peered across the way to see the narrow path winding its way uphill. Block-concrete walls sandwiched the path on either side so she couldn't see much, and on top of that, narrow side streets and stairways branched out like a maze. Looking far up the slope, she saw a towering stone wall and zigzagging steps crawling up it. It looked like there were even more villages on top of the wall.

She had heard that the old town around the transfer station had once been a military base in the Easterbury region. It was a fort city, surrounded by sturdy walls (though now they were old and crumbling in places), and even inside, it was divided by several layers of inner walls, which stood vertically, complicating the structure terribly. If someone who had never been there before entered the city and actually made it to their destination, there would be no doubt that it was pure coincidence.

Apparently Harvey had been there before. He did stop and look around a few times as if matching the streets with his memory, but he cut through several of the complex hill roads automatically and finally started down a single narrow path.

Old houses lined the run-down area. It looked as if hardly anyone lived there anymore; most of the houses within the crumbling concrete walls had fallen to ruin, and the yellow sand that had blown in from the wilderness lay thick on the streets.

Harvey stopped in front of one of the houses deep in the complex, and after gazing at it from the outside for a short while, he disappeared inside its concrete fence.

"He went inside."

At the radio's prompting, Kieli ran in his direction and, ducking low, stuck half her face out from behind the wall.

On the other side of the simple but well-maintained front yard, an old, steel-framed house stood under the evening sky. It was somewhat bigger than the other houses around it and had a stone stairway and double doors at its front.

Kieli was a little surprised to see potted herbs of various sizes lined up on the balcony directly above the front entrance. She had thought that the only people who could devote themselves to hobbies like raising plants these days were rich ladies in mansions who had a lot of free time because their servants did all the housework.

She saw the top half of a man on the balcony, watering the plants with a tin watering can. He was a white-haired old man who scowled grumpily, and at first glance, he certainly didn't look like someone who loved plants.

When he noticed Harvey looking up at him from outside the entrance, for a second he put a warning look on his face, then his eyes, buried in deep wrinkles, opened wide.

"You've come back. . . ." The minute the words reached his mouth, every trace of his previous stern expression melted away.

Kieli heard Harvey murmur, "I'm home." His voice was so faint that she didn't know if it reached the old man's ears or not.

"Don't just stand there; come in. It's your house," the old man called to Harvey and disappeared from the balcony, perhaps going to greet him. Accepting the invitation, Harvey started to climb the entrance steps but suddenly stopped and turned around.

"Ah," Kieli cried involuntarily as his copper-colored eyes met hers. Under her chin, the radio made the same sound. Harvey squinted at Kieli, who had frozen with her head still sticking out of the concrete's shadow, and sighed, an incredulous look on his face.

"I don't know what you're doing, or why you've even got the Corporal with you."

Kieli made the excuse in her mind — "It was the Corporal's idea" — but it stayed there.

"How long did you know?"

"The way Kieli tails people, I couldn't *help* but noticing. Kieli."

A little late, Kieli was trying to sneak her head back behind the wall; she cringed when he called her sharply by name. She looked up to check his expression, but Harvey simply said, "How about coming in?" He turned on his heels and pushed the double glass door open. The door creaked, terribly rusted.

Kieli's mouth dropped open. After looking down at the radio, she hurried out of the concrete's shadow and followed the tall man disappearing through the entrance.

She trotted up the steps but then, feeling as if something was off, she stopped. She looked up at the balcony above her and tilted her head. The terra-cotta pots were still there, but the herbs and their green leaves had all disappeared, as if perhaps someone had picked them all in an instant.

"Hey, this house . . ." she muttered, moving her gaze from the balcony across the entire house. The radio said only, "*I know*," in a deadpan voice, as if he had realized long before.

The inside of the house was all done in whites, and it was old, but clean. Inside, a hall surrounded by white walls stretched out in either direction. Harvey stuck his head out of one of the doors, said, "This way," and disappeared inside once again.

When she stood in front of the room Harvey beckoned her to, Kieli realized that this place was a facility like a clinic. In the center of the plain, undecorated room stood a simple bed and a medical cart, and the glass-doored cabinet that occupied one of the walls contained a variety of medicines.

There was a clumsy steel desk at the window, and the old man from earlier sat in front of it, looking her way.

"This is Kieli," Harvey said, introducing Kieli, who was standing in the doorway, then pulled a round chair from beside the bed, and sat casually in it. The crooked three-legged chair sank with a creak.

Kieli bowed her head slightly in acknowledgment, and the radio that hung from her neck introduced himself: *"I'm here, too."* The old man opened his eyes just a little wider in surprise, but soon looked pleased and smiled.

"Welcome. You seem to be pleasant companions. Are you happy?"

He directed the last question at Harvey, and Harvey, stuck for an answer, turned his glance toward Kieli. But it wasn't as if the answer would be written on her face. Kieli looked back at him silently, and eventually he smiled wryly and responded, "Well, things aren't so bad right now."

"Aren't so bad." It seemed to Kieli that when Harvey said it, it could fall into the category of "pretty good," and that was enough for her.

"Be careful. It looks like they'll give out any second."

"Yeah, I know." The radio didn't need to warn Kieli; she was already taking great care with each step up the staircase. The house seemed to be pretty old, and even her smallest steps made the floor creak.

While Harvey and the old man absorbed themselves in stories of the past, Kieli left the examination room and took a look around the clinic.

On the second floor, the balcony she saw from the gate was directly ahead of her, and a white hall lined with doors stretched out to her right and left, like on the first floor. Staring out of the corner of her eye at the green leaves that had returned to the pots on the balcony, she wandered down the hall to the right and peered through a few of the doors. One room after another was plain but clean-looking with one or two beds under the windows. The rooms were probably for inpatients.

"This is a nice place," the radio said quietly, and Kieli smiled and said, "Yeah."

There was no sign of extravagance, and while she couldn't deny its old age, a sense of cleanliness and a humble warmth filled every place she looked, and she could see what kind of a person ran the clinic. It was a quiet home, befitting someone who had the heart to care lovingly for potted plants on this world where there was nothing but rocky wilderness, oceans of quicksand, and exhausted coal mines.

She walked down the hall, feeling somehow that this place had healed even her, but she soon stopped in surprise.

Someone was at the hall's intersection. He was in front of the door farthest down the hall, clinging to the wall, and peering into the room. He looked like a little boy, even smaller than Kieli.

"Um . . . ?"

The minute she spoke to him, Kieli's consciousness was drawn inside the boy, and before she knew it, she was looking into the room from the boy's point of view.

It was a room with clean white walls, just like the others. A potted plant, different from the ones on the balcony, decorated the windowsill with its gentle green leaves.

There was a patient on the bed by the window. He was a young man Kieli knew well, with copper-colored hair. His hair was a little longer than now, and hopelessly unkempt. He sat up with his back against a pillow, but he leaned heavily to the left, apparently unable to use the right side of his body — or rather, half of it wasn't there. There was nothing filling his white shirt from the right shoulder down — only an empty sleeve dangled beside his body, and there was nothing under the sheet where his right leg should have been. He gazed at the half-done room with a vacant expression that suggested that half of his brain had fallen out as well, and he would blink only occasionally in response to the sounds outdoors that sometimes came through the window.

Kieli, overlapping the boy, observed him very cautiously from the door's shadow.

Be friends with him, Tadai.

Suddenly hearing a voice from behind her, she turned around and saw a man that looked much like the old man from earlier, but a little younger. *Father,* came to Kieli's lips. Then she felt a light push on her back and timidly went into the room. The youth on the bed moved very sluggishly and turned a somewhat unfocused gaze in her direction. Urged from behind by the father, she extended a hand — starting with her right but then switching to the left — to the young man. After a little time, he tried to raise his left hand, too, and that instant, he lost his balance and sank to the left. He kept going and fell off the bed.

She panicked and rushed to help him up, but she couldn't help laughing at such a magnificent fall; and then she got the feeling that the youth, whose empty expression hadn't shifted an inch until then, showed just a little smile. It was a really, really faint smile, but it was a smile.

When a sudden crash brought Kieli back to herself, she was standing alone inside the room. The boy and his father were both gone, and the bed was empty except for a white sheet.

"Corporal, did you see that . . . ?" she murmured, looking around the room. Under her chin, the radio answered simply, "*Yeah.*"

She heard another violent clatter from downstairs. Still a

little dazed, she went to the window and looked outside to see Harvey unceremoniously kick open the ill-fitted glass doors at the entrance and come out into the front yard.

"Are you going somewhere?" She tried to open the window, but there was no glass there to begin with, so Kieli just leaned out of it and called down to him. She'd be in trouble if he left her here.

The sky was gradually changing from the orange of dusk to the blue-gray of night, and the air had grown chill. The last rays of the sun cast long shadows on the yard, stretching Harvey's already-tall figure.

Harvey turned around to look up at her, and, a cigarette in his mouth, said, "For a smoke," in an unfriendly voice. It took Kieli a few seconds to figure out that he was going out into the yard to smoke a cigarette. "I'll get in trouble if I smoke inside. Smoking is strictly prohibited in the clinic," he added in explanation, responding to her blank stare. He smirked and ducked his head a little.

"Eh? But this house isn't . . ." Kieli started to protest, tilting her head in confusion. Then, "He's conscientious about strange things," a voice came from behind her. She turned to see the old man smiling wryly in the doorway. She stood rooted to her spot at the windowsill, at a loss for how to react. The old man took on a kind tone and said, "Would you like to see some old photographs?"

"I would!" Kieli immediately nodded vigorously. He smiled at her and disappeared into the hall, as if to say, "Follow me."

Before going after him, Kieli looked down from the window one more time. Harvey sat crouched on the steps outside the entrance, staring absently into the distant sky and puffing his cigarette. After making sure he was there, Kieli left the window.

By the time she went into the hall, the old man had already gone past the balcony and was standing on the opposite side of the hall, waiting in front of the door at the far end. Taking the utmost care not to make the floor creak, she ran after him, and the old man went inside the room, stood aside, and beckoned to Kieli.

This room felt more lived-in than the hospital rooms she had been looking at; it was packed with a disarray of furniture and seemed smaller. Unlike beds in the patients' rooms, with their tight white sheets, this bed was properly made up with a well-used brown blanket. It probably belonged to the old man himself.

A rusty picture frame decorated the end table beside the bed. Kieli hesitated a bit but then walked forward and gently picked it up. She felt the weight of the metallic frame in her hand.

The picture inside the frame showed three men: a middle-aged man and a young man with similar eyes who appeared to be father and son, and a youth with copper hair. She didn't know how many decades ago the faded photo had been taken, but in any case, it was old, and a Harvey completely unchanged from the one Kieli knew stood inside it.

She showed it to the radio that hung from its cord, near her stomach. *"The bastard really doesn't age,"* it muttered in exasperation. She thought Harvey wouldn't appreciate someone being exasperated about him.

Kieli felt a bit differently about it. The background in the photo looked a lot like the scene at the carnival they had visited the day before. She didn't know if it was the same town or another venue, but either way, they were in the middle of a festival, and Harvey was smiling innocently as he and the other young man had their arms around each other's shoulders, like best friends or brothers joking together.

She thought, *So Harvey can smile like this.* The Harvey Kieli knew was generally eighty percent expressionless and twenty percent either annoyed or bored. At the very most, she had seen him smile only wryly or faintly. When he smiled like this, he looked surprisingly childlike and seemed pretty warm.

After holding the frame tenderly and gazing down at the picture for a time, Kieli turned to look at the old man standing behind her.

"Is this you?" she asked, pointing at the middle-aged man who stood in the back, smiling gently as if watching over the two young men. The old man laughed and shook his head.

"That's my father. The one in front is me when I was younger," he said, pointing to the young man next to Harvey.

"Dad used to be a military doctor. He opened this clinic when the War ended and cared for people who were injured in the War. He was a hopeless philanthropist — he didn't just look after the injured but also worked with a charitable group that buried the heaps of corpses that were left behind on all of the ancient battlefields in Easterbury. He picked him up on his way back." He smirked as if to say, "literally picked him up." "He had been buried under a mountain of dead soldiers. At the time, I was very young, so when my dad told me to be friends with that half-dead corpse that he practically dug out of a grave, it was quite the shock."

The old man spoke in a mild voice that was easy to listen to, then narrowed his eyes, buried in wrinkles, as if in fond memory.

Oh, so that boy really was this old man. As she looked from the old man to the picture in her hand and back again, a warm feeling filled Kieli. That youth's face looked as if a big hole had opened up in his heart, but thanks to the boy and his father, he learned to smile like this.

"That was the last photograph. He left a little after it was taken." The old man's remark brought Kieli back to reality. Now that he mentioned it, Harvey said he had traveled all over the planet, so he couldn't have lived in this house forever.

She looked up from the picture and turned a questioning gaze to the old man. He closed his eyes and didn't answer immediately.

"If he was here long enough for that little boy to get as old as he is in this picture, he was already here plenty too long. It would be weird for the people around him not to get suspicious. The Church has a crazy reward out for the Undying; if you reported an Undying to the Church soldiers, you'd get enough money to buy a ship."

Kieli glanced down at the radio, then silently returned her gaze to the old man. He nodded, his eyes still closed.

"Dad died not long after that picture was taken. The direct cause was an old war wound that had gotten worse, but apparently he had been suffering a lot since Mom had gone before her time. After the funeral, *he* disappeared. And he never came back."

"Not even once?"

"Actually, we had been fighting," the old man said, laughing with a hint of self-contempt. Kieli stared at his face, a little surprised. Here he seemed like such a kind, gentle man, much like his father in the picture. It must have been Harvey's fault. Kieli started imagining a scene that, to Harvey, would be a baseless and false accusation.

"So you're saying that you may have owed my dad, but you don't owe me anything, and now that Dad's gone, there's no reason for you to stay, is that it?" This different voice suddenly interjected behind the old man.

She looked past the old man in surprise, and saw a tall shadow leaning against the door frame. For the first time, she noticed that her surroundings had gone completely dark, the faint bluish light from outside dimly illuminating the room's miscellaneous furniture.

"He yelled, and hit me as hard as he could. That sweet little old man was pretty hotheaded when he was young. Well, I appreciated that he had the guts to hit an Undying, so I didn't hit him back," Harvey said casually in the gloom. He raised one side of his mouth in a smirk, showing not an iota of the innocence of the smile in the picture.

Kieli threw him a supsicious glare, wondering where he'd picked up his current personality, and Harvey, ducking his head to let the glare pass, pointed toward the hall and downward.

"Kieli, do you mind if we stay here tonight? It's a little dusty, but I found a room on the first floor that I think you could sleep in."

Of course Kieli had no objections, so she nodded in assent. It was a shame not to stay at the inn they had already reserved in front of the station, but the only things she had were the shoulder bag she always carried with her and the radio (the radio technically belonged to Harvey, but somewhere along the way it had become the preferred style for Kieli to wear it around her neck).

"Then let's go. There's no electricity here, so we won't be able to see anything soon," Harvey urged her, disappearing from the doorway. Kieli glanced up at the old man next to her. He smiled bitterly and, nodding, stood up and left the room.

The last to leave, Kieli could see the backs of Harvey and the old man as they walked down the hall ahead of her, side by side. They argued about something as they went. The old man was half a head shorter than Harvey, but he was a match for him in attitude. "That was because you suddenly said you were leaving without giving any decent explanation. And Dad had just died; anybody would make that mistake."

"You shouldn't have needed an explanation to figure it out."

"Don't you get defiant on me! You've always been one extreme or the other — either you don't say enough or you say way too much. You need to learn a little consideration for who you're talking to."

"Augh, don't lecture me. I wasn't asking, damn it."

Walking behind them and staring at their backs, Kieli desperately tried to contain her laughter. *"What, are they little kids . . . ?"* the radio muttered in exasperation, but the Corporal had no right to talk about age or foul language, which made it even funnier, and Kieli giggled in the back of her throat.

The two of them are like best friends and brothers, just like the two joking around in the picture. I'm really glad they were able to talk again, she thought.

The next morning, when Kieli opened her eyes she was lying on a sofa with broken springs in the waiting room, wrapped in her coat and a dusty old blanket.

The clinic had completely fallen to ruin. Yellow sand and dust had settled below the crisp, clear, cold morning air, and the once clean, white paint on the walls had faded to yellow and peeled off in places, showing the concrete wall underneath.

Kieli spent a while walking through the deserted house, looking for Harvey, the floor creaking with every step she made. When she went up to the second floor, the plants that decorated the balcony had withered to nothing, and only the cracked pots remained under the nebulous morning light.

She stopped in front of the old man's room. There was no bedding on his mattress, and most of the furniture had been either broken or carried off, leaving the room empty. She walked to the end table and carefully picked up the photo frame that had been left facedown on top of it.

The photograph inside the rusted metallic frame had turned a milky white, and she could no longer make out anything except that there were three people in it.

"I'm sorry about dragging you along yesterday," a quiet voice addressed her from behind, and Kieli looked up from the photo. Harvey leaned in the door frame, just as he had done the night before. "Oh, no . . ." Kieli answered, shaking her head. Harvey smiled just a little more softly than usual.

"I'm going to visit his grave. Wanna come?"

There was an abandoned Church school in a corner of the upper level of the vertical inner wall that made the old city so complex, and the open lot next to it had become a public cemetery for the poor. The concrete walls that surrounded it were half-crumbled, and a cold but gentle morning breeze blew between the rows of stone grave markers.

In the farthest corner of the cemetery lay a simple tombstone belonging to the old man Kieli had met last night. It was covered in a layer of red dust that had come in from the wilderness, and it appeared that it had been there for at least a few years. Thinking about it, those memories in which the old man was a boy were right after the War ended, and that was almost eighty years ago.

Immediately next to his grave marker stood another that was a little older. Engraved on it was a modest epitaph, fitting of such a plain marker. "Here lies Tadius, beloved father of Harvey, Tadai, and many potted plants."

There was no inscription on the old man's grave; perhaps he had no family or close friends to care for him. There was another tombstone beside the father's grave. It was much more weathered than the other two, but she could just barely make out the words carved in it — "Here lies Harvey, most beloved son of Tadius, and Tadai's older brother."

Openmouthed, Kieli couldn't help staring at the letters on the tombstone.

"There was an elder son in that family," Harvey informed her in a smooth tone. "Apparently he died in battle six months before the war ended."

At a loss for words, Kieli looked up at Harvey, standing beside her. Harvey's profile wore no expression as he looked down at the grave, and he stood completely motionless for a while as he sometimes did, his eyes fixed downward. After waiting quietly for a while as Kieli hesitated to speak to him, he finally blinked once and turned his usual indifferent gaze toward her.

"I'm going to stay here a little longer. Would you go eat breakfast or something with the Corporal to kill time?"

"Can't I wait here . . . ?"

"No. Sorry, b . . ." Harvey started to say, then broke off as if the words were stuck in his throat. He showed a vague smile and averted his eyes. "But I want to be alone for a little while. . . ."

Kieli stood still for a time, looking at his face. She felt the inside of her throat tighten. She bit her lip and swallowed. *"Kieli, let's go,"* the radio's voice pressed her on, and she took two or three steps backward.

". . . Then I'll be off," she somehow managed to choke out, then turned on her heels and fled.

At the cemetery exit, she looked back and saw Harvey crouched on his knees in front of the grave. She faced forward again and ran at full speed, not looking back again. As she ran the inner wall's steps in one bound, the radio and her bag thudded against her.

An awkward, three-wheeled taxi with its cylindrical fuel tank on top drove sluggishly into the plaza in front of the station. It passed in front of the bench Kieli and the Corporal sat on, the fat muffler in the back spitting out black smoke that showed a severe lack of fuel efficiency, and Kieli, who was trying to take her first bite of breakfast, couldn't help choking.

"Kahah . . ."

As she coughed, she glared at the three-wheeled taxi as it continued into the rotary, caring not a bit that it had bothered her. A wealthy-looking couple with large bags stepped out of the taxi. The eastbound morning train would be arriving from the north soon, and from the bench in front of the plaza, she could watch as the station sucked up all the people who were ready to travel.

She didn't have much of an appetite, but she pulled herself together and started to eat again; her lunch was a bean sandwich she had bought at a junk-food stand in front of the station; it had sauteed beans and smashed vegetables pressed between hard bread. They would be walking a lot today, so she had resolved to make sure to eat. As she mused, something suddenly occurred to her, and she turned to the radio sitting next to her on the bench with her bag and asked, "Corporal, Harvey doesn't eat, does he?"

"*He eats,*" the radio answered readily, but in this case, Kieli's "eat" and the Corporal's "eat" didn't have quite the same flavor.

As of this morning, Kieli had been traveling with Harvey for four days, but she had never seen Harvey have a meal in all that time. No, like the radio said, she had seen him put things in his mouth, but it was always something like dried meat that seemed inedible to Kieli, or hardtack that was like rocks, and he gave the impression that he was thinking about something completely unrelated — just putting the food inside his mouth, chewing it up, and sending it down to his stomach — and when he got tired of it, he would stop. It was like he had no attachment whatsoever to the act of eating.

When she thought about it, as far as Kieli knew, she had never seen him sleeping, either. He would close his eyes, but if she talked to him, he'd immediately open them and answer her. He would just seem extremely annoyed about it.

I wonder if the Undying don't need to eat or sleep. Kieli had a hard time picturing what it would be like not to have to eat or sleep. Not sleeping meant that the world never pauses; there's no sense that today will end or tomorrow will come. She wondered what it would feel like to live in that monotonous routine for decades.

"All life functions for Undying are maintained by their hearts' unlimited power source, so they don't need to take any thought for how they live. That's how they get to be failures at life, like him." "Failure at life" was a really harsh way to put it, but it wasn't far off the mark. *"On top of that, their hearts give them blood with abnormal cell-regenerating powers that make them immortal. Convenient bastards."*

Kieli listened, fascinated, to the radio's half-ranting explanation as her molars ground up the hard-to-chew smashed vegetables from her bean sandwich.

She wondered if that strange coal-tar-like liquid that gathered around his wounds like a living thing contained something — something Kieli couldn't even imagine — that rapidly healed even fatal wounds. And it was the power source in his heart that sent it out — even Kieli could imagine this one. To be more precise, she could remember something she had seen with her own eyes. That rough black stone that was like a machine but also somehow not unlike a living thing.

"Those stones — the hearts of the Undyings — what in the world are they made of?"

"They say they're a crystallization of ultrapure energy sources. Before the War, they mined everywhere, getting a hell of a lot more highly pure fossil fuels than they can now, and built up an energy civilization on the planet. They gathered the essence of all that technology and made the Undyings' 'cores.' But they lost both the resources and the technology in the long War, and all that's left now is the scrap coal that moves those top-heavy clunkers."

She took in the radio's cynical comment and cast a glance at the rotary, where she could see a few three-wheeled taxis parked in a line, with huge fuel tanks sitting on their roofs, practically crushing them. She had learned some of the history of fossil fuels in school. An ugly war broke out over those resources, enveloping the entire planet, and when the resources dried up, the war naturally died out, too. Not only was it meaningless, but it wasted all kinds of labor on efforts that did nothing but harm and brought destruction over the entire planet.

The area surrounding the station's entrance suddenly got very busy. Apparently the train had arrived, and flocks of people came flowing outside as if pushed along. The taxi drivers, who were camping out around the ashtrays in the rotary, smoking, instantly exchanged their bored expressions for courteous smiles and started hunting for customers.

Kieli gazed emotionlessly at the activity in front of the station and kept chewing her breakfast; by the time she finished, both the arriving and departing passengers had settled down and the flow of people had thinned. The lucky taxis that had apprehended passengers with deep pockets passed in front of her, spewing black smoke and noise as usual.

She scowled at the exhaust fumes as she swallowed the last bite of her bean sandwich, and just then, she happened to catch sight of a three-wheeled taxi coming her way.

That instant, the taxi's front wheel suddenly changed direction and charged toward the bench Kieli and the Corporal were sitting on.

"Waah!" Kieli screamed, reflexively pulling her legs up onto the bench. Fortunately, the front wheel swerved in the opposite direction in the nick of time, and after tottering from side to side for a while as if the driver was drunk, the taxi came to a sudden stop a little ways off. The driver leapt out, his face pale, and looked around at his car and its surroundings, then got back inside, shaking his head in confusion.

"There was something on top of it . . ." Kieli muttered, still a little dazed and clinging to the back of the bench she had scrambled onto as she gazed at the black smoke coming from the taxi as it left the station. For just a second, she had seen a fuzzy black shadow riding on the fuel tank on the roof and blocking the windshield.

"A nasty evil spirit making mischief. Best not to get involved," the radio replied, not particularly concerned. But in a somewhat stiffer voice, he added, *"We'd better get going, just in case. Let's go back to Herbie."*

"Yeah . . ." Kieli nodded tentatively, but still followed the direction the taxi had taken with her eyes as she slowly lowered her feet from the bench to the ground. She hoped there wouldn't be any big accidents.

"Kieli. Yo, let's go. I'm the one who'll get smashed to pieces if you get hurt while Herbie's not around."

"Yeah . . ." she responded halfheartedly to the voice that sounded annoyed as it urged her on. Then, "Eh? What do you mean?" she asked, stunned, before the spectacular noise of a fossil-fueled engine jumped to her ears.

She looked up in surprise; a different taxi, the same model as the one from before, drove up the street in front of her, then made a ninety-degree turn and entered the station's front area. As expected, the same black shadow possessed the fuel tank and was hanging upside down from the roof, peering through the windshield. The taxi veered right and left, but for some reason, no one hit the brakes as it charged ahead at breakneck speed.

At the end of its projected path, she saw a traveler walking along absentmindedly and carrying a large bag, as if he had just come out of the station.

"Look out!" Kieli yelled, at the same time kicking off from the bench in a run. She caught the traveler's clothes and barely managed to pull him to the curb in time, but he lost his balance and fell into her, and they both tumbled onto the ground. His travel bag flew out of his hands, clattering loudly as it hit the pavement. The taxi spouted exhaust menacingly, as if yelling at them to get out of the way, as it immediately sped off down the road.

Still on her rear end on the asphalt, Kieli watched, appalled, as the taxi broke the speed limit. It stopped suddenly in front of the station, and a fat, self-important-looking man jumped out, shouting self-importantly, but that wouldn't help him catch his train. *Ugh, that was close. Serves you right.*

She shifted her hateful gaze upward and saw the evil spirit floating in the air above the runaway taxi, looking over the rotary with a faint smile on its shadowy face. It had only the top half of a body, with abnormally long arms dangling at its sides. The lower half of its body trailed off into the air and vanished.

When Kieli then turned to look at the traveler who had fallen onto the curb beside her, her jaw dropped and she stared at his profile. She got the feeling that the traveler was directing his eyes at the evil spirit floating in the air, too.

"Um . . ." she started to address him, but his gaze quickly moved, as if he hadn't been looking at anything in particular. He stood up, brushed the dust off his clothes with one hand, and offered her the other. Kieli froze, dumbfounded, so he took her arm himself and helped her up.

"Thank you."

"No, I should be thanking you." The traveler expressed his gratitude in a soft tone and smiled sweetly. Standing next to him, Kieli saw that he was a young man about the same height as Harvey, and her heart skipped a beat when she got the feeling that he resembled Harvey somehow. In an effort to hide her reaction, she brushed the dust off her skirt, turning her eyes upward to look at the traveler. That was when she first realized that he was no ordinary traveler. He wore pitch-black priest's garb of fine quality — the clothes of a priest on pilgrimage.

She wondered why she had thought he resembled Harvey for a second: now that she looked at him, other than his apparent age and height, he wasn't really like Harvey at all. He was an honest-looking young man, whose blue-gray eyes radiated a gentle aura.

"From your uniform, I'd say you're a student at the Easterbury boarding school." Apparently while Kieli inspected the priest, he had been inspecting her. He looked down at Kieli's black garments and asked in surprise, "Traveling alone in uniform?"

"Uh, it's a research trip. And I'm not alone . . ." Kieli answered automatically (until she said it, she had completely forgotten about the report herself) and glanced over at her companion on the bench. Then she almost cried out.

She hadn't seen the half-bodied evil spirit approach, but suddenly it was floating in the air above the radio, a mischievous smile showing faintly on its face. Static particles spewed out of the radio, forming a fuzzy soldier's face, which looked overhead and opened its mouth menacingly.

Waah, Corporal! Kieli screamed inside her head. "I'm sorry, I'm in a hurry! Good-bye!" She bid farewell to the priest without giving him a chance to respond, ran back to the bench, snatched up her bag and the radio, and raced away from the station without giving the evil spirit or the priest another look.

"There — done . . ." Harvey muttered to himself, lowering the knife in his hand. He rested his chin on his bent knee and gazed at his handiwork for a while, rather pleased with himself.

The blank tombstone now had letters engraved on it, though not particularly well. "Here lies Tadai, son of Tadius; younger brother, older brother, and first friend of Harvey."

"Well, you'll just have to make do with this," Harvey told the grave, then smiled wryly at the ridiculousness of his own action. But there was a little more he wanted to make sure to say out loud.

"Right now, my life's generally not so bad, so don't worry about me. I enjoy what I can wherever I am, and I have someone who's making life good. But . . ." As he spoke, he crossed his arms over his knee and buried his face.

"I'm fed up with it already. Just imagine, every single person I meet up with dies, leaving me behind. Even you. You don't even care how the hell I feel. *You're* satisfied, so you just go and die."

His brother under the grave marker would no longer respond like he had the night before. Even so, he waited, hoping somewhere in his heart for something, but all he could hear was the dry sound of the wind carrying the dust and yellow sand that piled up on the ground.

"Hmph, so no one's coming to take me away after all?" he spat, with a short sigh, then brushed away the dust and stood up. He looked down once more at the newly engraved tombstone, offered a short prayer, then lifted his eyes and turned away. If they didn't leave soon, they wouldn't make it to the ruins before sunset. He felt hesitant about making Kieli camp out.

". . . Well, I guess it's still all right . . ." he muttered before leaving the grave. It was more to himself than to his brother sleeping there.

"Kieli! Hey, Kieli, stop! I'm gonna fall apart! I'm rickety enough as it is!" The radio's protests were close to screams. Kieli finally stopped running. The radio had been flailing at the end of the cord in her hand as she raced at full speed.

Catching her breath, she took a look at her surroundings. She had escaped the plaza in front of the station, and the next thing she knew, she was already inside the old city.

It was already pretty late in the morning, but there were very few passersby. Even the trash strewn across the streets looked weathered, as if the town had given up on the idea of cleaning long ago, and a somehow resigned mood hung in the air. Thanks to the nature of transfer stations, the new town around the station flourished regardless of its remote location, but just a little way away, the place became an old, abandoned ghost town, like the neighborhood around Easterbury's old station.

"Oh, that scared me. It would have been big trouble if you had gone on a rampage back there," Kieli whispered in a subdued voice as she returned the radio and her bag to their normal positions and walked resolutely toward the public cemetery.

"*I was just threatening him a little to get him to go away. Besides, he came up to me first.*"

"You're the one that said it's best not to get involved with spirits like that, Corporal," she responded, pursing her lips. The radio groaned and said vaguely, "*Never mind that,*" forcing the conversation in another direction.

"*It's good that it got you away from that guy. Of course I feel the same about that evil spirit, but something about that guy just really bugs me. It's best not to get involved with him either.*"

"Why?" His sudden warning shocked Kieli, and she looked down at the radio as it swung against her stomach in time with her footsteps.

"*Something felt weird about him.*"

"What did?"

"*Just something. I was trying to get a better idea when that annoying spirit came up to me.*"

"So basically there's no reason. *I* thought he was nice."

She tried to remember the priest's face, but he hadn't really left an impression on her except that he had pretty blue-gray eyes that matched the night sky, and that for some reason, he reminded her of Harvey for a second. But she at least didn't get the impression that he was a bad man.

The radio seemed to want to say more, but convinced himself, "*Oh well, we'll never see him again. We're leaving this town,*" bringing the conversation to a close.

"Yeah," Kieli replied only briefly, and shut her mouth for a while.

If they walked all day, they would reach the ruins that evening. Before she knew it, their destination was right in front of them. Kieli became aware of that fact and suddenly started to worry about what would happen after they got there. It had seemed so far off, she didn't have much of a sense that the time would come — no, maybe, unconsciously, she was trying not to think about it.

There wasn't much left of the Colonization Days vacation. When they returned from the ruins, Kieli would have to go back to the boarding school, although not even Becca would be there anymore when she got back. What would Harvey do after returning the Corporal to his grave . . . ?

"Um, hey. When we get to the ruins, we'll have to say goodbye, won't we?" she asked hesitantly as she turned down a side street in the direction of the public cemetery. After a short silence, the radio answered, *"Yeah."* She couldn't tell him she didn't want to. Not if it was what the Corporal wanted and if it was natural for dead people, like it was for Becca.

She left the narrow, paved byroad and started up the staircase that zigzagged up the inner wall. At the top was the abandoned Church school, and the lot next to that was the old city's public cemetery.

"Wha?"

Right as she passed the landing on the highest level, something suddenly yanked her neck from behind, and she automatically let out a cry as the air rushed out of her throat. Surprised that she had stopped breathing for a moment, she turned her head behind her.

Two long arms appeared impossibly in the air and were trying to take the radio that hung from her neck — to be more accurate, they were trying to drag out the spirit that was possessing the radio.

"Let go, damn it!" the soldier yelled, the top half of his body having been pulled out of the floating radio. Kieli's legs swam in the air as she was pulled backward with the radio. Before she could react, her back hit the concrete stairs, and she slid backward down a few steps to the landing below.

"Kgh . . ." she cried wincing at the pain in her back, then sat up and looked to her left and right. The radio had come off her neck, and she could see it banging against the pavement as it rolled down the stairs.

"Corporal!" Despite the pain, Kieli stood up and hurried after the radio. She got impatient and started skipping steps, running with such force that it seemed any wrong step would send her tumbling down the stairs, too; but anyway, she ran.

The radio bounced high with a dull thud. Kieli reached out with all her might to grab its cord, but there was no stair for her foot to land on.

"Ahhh — !"

She curled up instinctively, but this time she fell past the landing and all the way to the bottom, stopping when she crashed onto the pavement in the alley below. ". . . gh!" A moment later, an intense pain attacked her shoulder joints, and she let out a scream that had no voice.

"Kieli!" the radio's call hit the back of her head as she cringed, unable to move from the pain. Its voice immediately changed into a furious roar. She managed to look up to see the half-bodied spirit floating above the radio on the ground in front of her. Its long arms wrapped around the Corporal's spirit body as it tried to pull him out of the radio.

"What do you think you're you doing? Let go!" When the Corporal bellowed, the radio's speaker swelled to a dome shape and started shooting out shock waves that looked like

condensed air. The evil spirit floated out of the way to a higher elevation, and the air-splitting shock wave crashed into the alley wall, crumbling the concrete.

Drifting in the air, the evil spirit curled its mouth into a half-moon, clearly laughing at them. Pieces of broken concrete shook noisily, as if laughing with it; they rose up to the evil spirit's eye level, forming a rough circle. "Corporal, run!" Kieli cried in spite of herself, knowing that she was saying the impossible, when she saw the projectiles aimed at the radio on the ground.

The evil spirit glared at her in irritation; as it did, the projectiles changed the target of their attack toward her, and when the evil spirit gave the signal with its eerily long fingers, they all commenced their assault.

Kieli couldn't react right away; her eyes widened and stared above her, still sitting on the ground. Pieces of concrete as big as her head formed groups that plunged toward her.

A moment too late, she closed her eyes tight, and the second she had half-resigned herself to her fate, someone's arm scooped her up from the side, and her feet floated in the air. Surprised, she opened her eyes again. Peripherally, she saw pieces of concrete piercing the ground where she lay seconds before as she was gently released a few meters away.

"Harve . . ." Unable to grasp the situation, she looked up at the owner of the arm that had rescued her, still a little dazed. Harvey only said shortly, "You okay?" in her ear, then turned his neck and cast his eyes toward the air above them. The evil spirit twisted its face in annoyance and spun around as if to tell them they'd spoiled its mood by getting in the way of its fun.

"Stay here. I'll be right back," Harvey said in a low voice, still glaring overhead. He shook off Kieli's hand and stood up. *"Herbie!"* the radio yelled, lying on the ground a little ways off.

Harvey snatched up the radio's cord as he ran past and went after the retreating spirit.

Running down the sloping alley, Harvey fixed his gaze on the half-bodied ghost's back as it drifted away. Around the radio, the Corporal's staticky face howled. The speaker produced a shock wave that went after the spirit, but it just barely missed its target and dispersed in the air.

The spirit turned and disappeared through a wall; by the time Harvey jumped out of the alley after it, it was already gone. "Corporal, stop," he commanded the radio in a low voice, as it was all set to release another shock wave, and stopped where he stood.

They had come out into the old city's main street, and people were walking about.

"*What the hell was that? Coming at me for no reason,*" the radio spat, peeved, as it dangled from Harvey's hand.

"You probably had him intrigued, Corporal," Harvey answered vaguely, keeping his guard up for a while as he watched for any signs of the spirit from the corner of the alley, but apparently it was no longer in the neighborhood.

"It got away . . ."

"*Damn it, another spectacular failure. Even I'm amazed I've lasted this long. Anything else happens, and I'll be scrap for sure.*"

The radio continued his endless complaints, but Harvey responded casually, "You only need that body for today anyway. Just in case, let's get out of here now," and turned on his heels, inwardly muttering, "He likes that body more than he lets on."

As he started back toward the road they had come from, he thought he felt eyes on them and stopped for a moment. He turned around and directed his gaze at the sparse traffic on the main street, but there were only residents of the old town walking listlessly by, and nothing really caught his eye. Apparently he had imagined it.

Harvey jogged up the sloping alley; when he got halfway up, he saw a girl walking slowly down the slope, using the wall for support. "I thought I told you to wait," he hurried up to her.

"You okay, Kieli? Sorry about that," the radio asked, concerned.

"I'm fine. It wasn't your fault, Corporal," Kieli replied with a smile, but scratches showed here and there on her slender hands and legs, which appeared even whiter against her black uniform. Her bruises were probably even worse. The bag she wore had slipped a little from her recently injured shoulder.

"Give me that," Harvey said shortly, holding his hand out to Kieli. Kieli just stared up at him blankly, so he breathed a small sigh and took the bag off her shoulder.

"So you can be a gentleman when you try."

"Shut up. I'm always a gentleman," Harvey snarled in response to the radio's quip, holding it up to his eyes and glaring at it as he hung Kieli's bag from his own shoulder with his other hand. "Damn it, and you were with her. Anything happens again, and *I'll* be the one to turn you into scrap."

"Heh. Too bad for you, *I'm only in this body for today anyway,"* the radio replied, not to be outdone. Harvey glowered at it as if to say, "That was *my* line," and then noticed Kieli staring at him.

"What? Are you hurt? Want me to carry you?" he asked, wincing somewhat; when she gazed at him with her honest, black eyes, he felt an inexplicable sense of guilt. Kieli hung her head and shook it back and forth, and after a moment muttered hesitantly, "It's not that. Are *you* okay, Harvey?"

"Me?" Harvey repeated automatically, then, ". . . Oh, am *I* okay? That's stupid. Don't worry about me." He almost made a face resembling a bashful smile, then panicked and went back to his normal scowl. "If you can walk, then let's go," he said over his shoulder as he turned and walked away in an effort to hide his display of emotion.

Walking at a slower pace than usual, matching the footsteps of the girl following behind, he groaned inwardly. He had thought he was the one looking after her, but before he knew it, it was her existence that was rescuing him.

The first order he heard was to go to Easterbury because a cat had been hit by a train and the body was nowhere to be found. After asking what on earth the problem was, he was forced to listen to a few meaningless complaints (as if he gave a damn about their grandkids' future schooling problems). He finally reached the heart of the matter — he was to go investigate the black tarlike bloodstains found at the scene of the accident. Why didn't they just say so? Clearly they had things all out of order.

"*What? You're still at the transfer station? What are you wasting time there for? Get to Easterbury and go after that Undying.*"

"I'm terribly sorry. I wasn't feeling very well, so I got a late start. I don't have any pleasant memories of the area around Easterbury."

"*Huh. I can't imagine you'd have pleasant memories of anywhere.*"

Inwardly sneering, "I don't need your commentary," he outwardly answered very politely, "Oh, please don't say that. Thanks to my delay, I have some good news to report. I've already found him without having to go all the way there."

"*What's that?*"

"The Undying was at the transfer station. Considering the time elapsed and the distance traveled, he's probably the same one who was in Easterbury. He's an acquaintance of mine, though I never thought I would find him here."

"Oh? Who is he? Where is he headed?"

"A detestable man named Ephraim. He's completely un-friendly." He could feel the vomit rise to his throat just from speaking the name. "He went south along the abandoned rail-road. The only thing in that direction is the abandoned mine."

"Understood. Finish the job there. I'll send some cars for backup," he said and hung up, not waiting for an answer.

". . . Yeah, yeah," he said derisively to the man on the other end, who could no longer hear him. He turned off the trans-mission from his end and cursed as he rudely knocked the six-inch blacked-out monitor to the ground. He composed himself a bit and thought, *Idiot Church leaders; I pretend to be a little submissive, and they get carried the hell away. I could kill them any time,* as he bent down in his priest robes and picked up the transmitter. It might be broken, but it didn't matter; he could just get a new one.

It would seem that chance encounters sometimes bring with them wonderful good luck. Accident-causing evil spirits weren't all that uncommon, but girls carrying possessed ra-dios weren't something he saw every day. He watched her for a while, intrigued, and then who should appear but that Ephraim. *Hmm. So he was still alive. That color — his eyes are as disgusting as ever.*

His nausea returned and he spat at his feet, but suddenly, a faint smirk came to his lips. He had an idea.

To think that that girl is traveling with Ephraim. Well then, when I finish this job, he won't mind if I take her.

CHAPTER 5

THE DEAD SLEEP IN THE WILDERNESS

Crunch, clunk. Crunch, clunk. . . .

She walked along the rusty train tracks, treading alternately on ballast and railroad ties. Sometimes the pace changed and they had snippets of conversation here and there, but for the most part, she walked in silence for hours, listening only to the monotonous sound of her own footsteps.

It was the time of day when the sand-colored gas on the horizon began to take on the reddish hue of dusk. Kieli's long, thin shadow stretched to several times her original height and extended over the dry earth from west to east.

The train track continued directly south, perpendicular to that shadow.

The ruined railroad was no longer in use, but it was said that it was a relic from before the war, when the planet was still rich in resources and trains had run along it, carrying the resources excavated from the mines to the center of civilization.

"We're almost there," the radio muttered, swinging at the end of its cord.

"Yup, we're almost there," Kieli echoed. The conversation was without purpose, and silence fell once again. Thick gravelly saliva clung to the inside of her mouth because she had been walking for so long; she figured that was why she wasn't talking as much.

Harvey, walking a little ahead of her, suddenly stopped and turned halfway around. He waited in that position for Kieli to catch up to him, then tossed the canteen to her. She caught the rusty silver-colored canteen in both hands and sent him a dubious look. His eyes didn't show any expression in particular as he asked, "What?"

"Oh, nothing," Kieli answered, then drank the dirty water gratefully, despite its rusty, sandy taste.

She didn't know what had caused his change in behavior. When they walked from the train wreck to the town with the carnival, he walked relentlessly on ahead without changing his pace. But today, he would sometimes stop and wait for her. The bag that Kieli usually wore on the shoulder that got hit on the stairs that morning was now hanging with Harvey's backpack from one of his shoulders.

"Once we get through there, it'll be right there," Harvey said, throwing a glance in the direction they were headed. Ahead of them, Kieli could see a rocky mountain range rising like a giant wave advancing on the wilderness. The railroad ran straight toward a tunnel dug into the rocks.

As the tunnel sank into darkness, Harvey's portable light illuminated their surroundings. They were rock walls, but humans had taken their hands to them; broken lights hung at angles, and bent pipes crawled along the walls. No wind blew in from the wilderness; instead, a penetrating cold stagnated throughout the tunnel, and Kieli huddled inside her coat, feeling it was even more wintry than it had been outside.

Taking care not to trip on the railroad at her feet, she followed Harvey's back deeper into the tunnel. Suddenly, a black train charged in front of her, without the chugging sound that usually came with it.

"Kya . . . !" All Kieli could do was let out a short scream; she couldn't move. For a second, the image of the train hitting her and knocking her broken body into the wall ran through her head.

However, the train didn't turn Kieli into a lump of meat but penetrated her body and kept on running. Kieli had the strange experience of passing through the inside of a train while standing still on its track.

It wasn't a passenger train with its familiar boxed seats — there were only simple seats installed on either side of the long, narrow cars, and people in work clothes jammed tightly into them. The passengers slumped their shoulders and hung their heads in exhaustion. Their pale faces passed by, nearly touching Kieli's cheeks as they went, and she even got the feeling her eyes met with a few of theirs at point-blank range.

After the passenger cars, she passed through the insides of the freight cars, packed with fossilized resources. A curious scene passed rapidly by, as if she had become a microbe and crawled between the rocks.

Her field of vision suddenly opened up, and she realized that the train had gone; she looked behind her to see the train waver and disappear at the tunnel's exit.

"Wh . . . what was that . . . ?"

"The proverbial ghost train." Harvey commented on the very unusual event as if it was the most ordinary thing in the world as Kieli stood there, watching the train vanish.

"Gho . . ." Speechless, Kieli turned her head back around. Harvey acted even more indifferent to these things than usual; he seemed to be thinking about something as he looked around at the rock walls.

"I'm surprised. There's still plenty *of ultrapure stuff left in this layer of the planet,"* the radio said, sounding impressed. Kieli just blinked, not knowing what he meant, so he explained.

"It's easy for spirit energy to stagnate in the magnetic field created in strata of this planet by fossilized resources. Especially in tunnels. Spirits like that one just now were witnessed on a daily basis. But the ultrapure fossil resources dried u . . . special qualities of the strata natural . . . fade . . ." During the second half of his explanation, the Corporal's voice became terribly staticky and started breaking up. Kieli looked down in surprise and saw that the particles from the speaker were trying to form the soldier's face but dispersed weakly as if something erased them.

"Corporal? What's wrong?"

"I'm fine. Spirits are easily affected by the influence of these strata. . . . I'm a . . . little un . . . stable, is all."

Becoming anxious, Kieli held the radio in her arms and threw a glance at Harvey. "Harvey, the Corporal's . . ." she started to say, then stopped short.

Harvey casually raised his hand above his head and placed it on the rock wall, and there was a small sound like a gauge needle going outside its range. His hair flew up, as if hit by a wind blowing from his feet.

She got the feeling Harvey's expression stiffened for just a second, but when he turned around and said, "I'm fine. Let's hurry and get out of here," he had returned to his usual emotionless demeanor.

The tunnel went on much longer than she thought, and as they went deeper inside, the noise from the radio grew worse.

"Are you okay, Corporal?"

"Yeah . . ."

She didn't know if spirits could feel pain, but the radio's voice was weak. Kieli embraced the radio with both arms and wondered if they might never reach the exit. Her anxiety spurred her on, and she walked on through the long, narrow darkness, guided only by Harvey's silent back.

A long, narrow, enclosed space. A tunnel.

Something tugged at Kieli's memory.

"Ah!"

It was the dream she had before the train accident, the one about the battle. When she looked up with a gasp, the scene that leapt to her eyes made Kieli scream convulsively.

Suddenly a crowd of people surrounded her, and they were all headed in the same direction. They were soldiers, wearing ragged uniforms. Many of them were injured, and dragged themselves along, using their rifles and sabers as support, but frantically pressing on toward the exit.

"Harvey . . ." Holding the radio tightly, Kieli called out pleadingly to the figure that walked ahead of her.

"This is a scene created by the memories of the soldiers that died at that time, being sewn over this tunnel. It's nothing to worry about," Harvey said in a cool, or rather, monotone voice, without looking back or stopping.

"Retreating soldiers ran into the mine up ahead in the final stages of the war. These are the soldiers that died then. We're heading for the war ruins; it's nothing to be surprised about," he added curtly, and Kieli could no longer ask for any relief. She cast frightened glances to her right and left, and decided that, anyway, they had better get out of this tunnel, and sped up after Harvey.

Perhaps the magnetic field in the rock walls affected the spirit matter, because sometimes the soldiers looked fuzzy as they walked forward, hunched over. Kieli and Harvey passed through them quickly.

Just then, a few soldiers started to run, practically falling over, afraid of something.

The panic spread in an instant. Those who could move started to run, and those who couldn't run were knocked down and trampled under waves of people. Kieli thought it strange that they all seemed to be running away from something behind them, and she started to turn around.

"*They're here! The bastards are here!*" The radio's scream beat through its speaker.

"Corporal? What? What's the matter?" This was the first time Kieli had heard the Corporal's voice so scared, and she looked down in surprise at the radio in her arms. The speaker spit out static particles like swarms of black insects that immediately disappeared. The chaos increased as the soldiers around them tried harder to escape.

"Turn me off, Kieli! Turn off my power until we get through here!" his voice shouted, mixed with so much noise that it made her want to cover her ears. Kieli let out a short scream and dropped the radio. The radio swung around on its cord.

"Turn him off! Now!" came a sharp command from in front of her. With it came Harvey's hand, which forcefully turned off the power.

The soldiers were still in the midst of their panic, but with the radio's static gone, the sound, at least, went quiet. She looked around blankly at the mismatched scene of people running around in silence. ". . . eh?"

She saw Harvey's tall frame lurch over in the corner of her eye. He put one hand against the wall and pressed the other around his heart. "What's wr —" She went to him and peered up into his face. When she thought about it, she got the feeling she had not seen Harvey's face once since they started walking through the tunnel; now that she did, she could tell even in the darkness how much blood had drained from it. His fingers clutched the clothes at his chest so tightly they could tear his skin off.

"Oh, no. Hey, do you hurt somewh —"

"Never mind. I'll be fine when we get out of here. Let's go."

Kieli clung to him in shock. Harvey shook her off and supported himself on the wall as he started walking. Kieli unconsciously looked around for help, but of course no one was there, and all she saw was the chaos of the retreating soldiers getting worse and worse.

Something was coming from behind.

"Don't look, Kieli."

By the time Harvey's voice tried to stop her, she was already looking back the way they had come.

A soldier who had been running right behind her overshadowed her, his eyes wide and his mouth open in a cry of death. He kept going through Kieli and fell to the ground. A saber protruded from his back. As the hand that held its hilt effortlessly removed the blade, blood gushed from the soldier's body and splattered Kieli's face.

She looked up in terror, and the "enemy" stood unsteadily before her, the saber dangling in one hand. His face had been blurry in the dream she had before, but now she could make it out clearly.

A young soldier looked down at her with empty, copper-colored eyes.

"Harvey . . . ?"

The "enemy" in front of her raised his saber toward the retreating soldier that now overlapped Kieli in his escape. Without a moment's hesitation, he swung it down on Kieli's head.

"Stop!" Harvey yelled, waving his arms wide to brush it away. As his clenched fists hit the layer of rock wall, shaking the air, the image of the "enemy" wavered and disappeared.

Kieli froze for a few seconds, gaping at the empty space where the "enemy" had been. When Harvey slid down the wall and collapsed onto his knees, she snapped out of her daze and ran to him, crouching beside him.

". . . op." Harvey was muttering something under his breath as he knelt on the ground, holding his pale face in one hand. When she leaned close, she heard him repeating, "Stop!" When she touched his back, it was trembling.

"Harvey . . ."

Kieli bit her lip, pulled herself together, and wrapped both arms around his back. "Let's get out of here. Let's hurry and get out of here. I'll take you."

She crawled under his large body and somehow managed to start dragging him along the tunnel.

She could see the exit in the distance. The soldiers who had succeeded in passing Kieli and escaping to the outside wavered and disappeared, just like the ghost train. Beyond the exit, a deep blue-gray painted the night sky, and she saw something resembling a train platform floating palely a little way outside.

One of them launched an unexpected counterattack. He should have run out of bullets long ago, but he must have had some hidden away and launched another barrage. *If you've got bullets, use them before you lose, stupid.* There was a dull crunch as a bullet hit him directly in the face and gouged out one of his eyeballs.

"Urgh . . ." All he did was mutter meaninglessly and put a hand to his sunken face. Now the gun really had run out of bullets, and the soldier froze in place. He stepped in front of him and slashed his saber at the soldier.

The soldier's chest split open, exposing his internal organs, and he fell flat on his back.

"Monster . . ." By the time he spat his last word, along with the blood that overflowed from his throat, he was already dead. He was a one-legged man with sunken cheeks and two blue stars on his sleeve, indicating that he held the rank of corporal — not that it mattered.

"This won't cut anymore." He frowned at the blood-encrusted saber, its blade now completely useless, and tossed it aside. He undid the clasp on the bayonet strapped to his back.

"How many did you kill, Ephraim?" Joachim asked him, standing to his right. What a depressing and annoying question. "That's a depressing and annoying question," Jude said from his left, and Joachim twisted his cheeks into an odd shape, his feelings apparently hurt. He was a depressing and annoying guy. Who cared how many he killed?

Bodies of retreating soldiers lay in heaps in their wake, burying the railroad track. Even if they did make it out of the tunnel, their enemies had nowhere to escape and no way to resist. They merely had to kill them all.

They did kill them all, and the War ended.

And then, there was no longer any need for them to exist. What was needed instead was someone to take responsibility for the War, and the entire planet tried to force the blame onto everyone else, starting with the Church. In the end, the thankless role and all of the negative feelings that caused future generations to remember their war-torn past fell on *them* and everyone like *them*.

Thus the legend of the "Demons of War" came into being after the War, and a branch of Church Soldiers put on their imposing armor and formed a squadron known as the Undying Hunters.

And before they knew it, it was their turn to be killed.

"Scatter! Ephraim, Joachim!" Jude shouted his low, sharp command, and they retreated from the train tracks to the wilderness where a gap cut perpendicularly through the rocks. The Church's armored car charged along the tracks; after going a little too far, it spouted a puff of smoke and came to a sudden stop. Church Soldiers wearing white armor filed out, carrying unfamiliar, high-caliber guns.

At the edge of his vision, he could see Jude coming to a halt; he looked back as he ran. Jude glanced at him and motioned with his hand for him to hurry on. Concentrated fire showered the top half of his body, and in the blink of an eye Jude was enveloped in black smoke and dust.

"Jude!" He automatically stopped and started to reverse direction; Joachim only gave him a sideways glance and kept running, not even slowing down. Depressing and annoying.

In the split second he sent a glare at Joachim, a line of bullets hit the side of his face.

"Damn it . . . !" The right half of his body was blown away completely as he escaped, practically falling into the shadows of the steep rocks.

He didn't know how or where he ran after that, but the next thing he knew, the mazelike rock shelf opened up onto a wilderness, and he was crawling through the ruins of an old battlefield. He crept along the ground, dragging himself forward with only his left arm, having lost more than half of the right side of his body. The fingernails he dug into the hard earth had already come off, and he no longer had any feeling in his fingertips.

He couldn't tell if he had fought on this battlefield. The stench of blood that permeated the air and earth had long since dried up, and the wind blew up the dust very close to the ground and carried it off. Weathered corpses lay in piles that went on endlessly in the red clay wilderness.

He was exhausted to the core of his being; nothing mattered anymore. Jude was probably already dead. It would be nice if Joachim had done him the favor of dying somewhere, too. Figuring it would be easiest to just rot along with the mountains of corpses, he stopped moving forward.

But he lay there for days, still conscious, and every single night, the dead bodies on the field came to express their hatred at length. Weeks passed, and the armored bugs that crawled through the wilderness crept into his skin and ate away at his flesh; even when they left, tiny wounds like those would heal by the next day, and of course he would be their dinner again. And the corpses came to talk to him as usual. No one would let him sleep.

Spending hundreds of days gazing at nothing but a vast ocean of cadavers, he started thinking that this must be his punishment. It must have been that he had taken the lifetimes of all the people he had killed, which no doubt meant he had a long time forced onto him to reflect on his actions — so long that he couldn't see the end of it. And to get to the end of it, whatever he did, he had no time to sleep.

At the very least, he would make sure not to take anyone's life again. It was tiring to live long enough for someone else. He wished he could give the time back to the people he had killed and have them forgive him. . . .

Harvey heard faint music. It was one of the radio's favorites, an upbeat melody that he had recently gotten thoroughly sick of hearing. But the volume was turned down so as not to be too loud, and the staticky sound of the stringed instruments actually brought a comfortable relief from the surrounding silence.

He felt cold asphalt under his back, and when he opened his eyes, the deep blue-gray that lay heavily over the night sky covered his vision.

He had more or less regained consciousness and was able to comprehend the situation. There was a weather-beaten station just outside the tunnel, and he was lying on its platform. A girl with a small build had flopped down beside him and appeared to be listening to the radio she held in her lap, but feeling his gaze, she turned to look at him.

Still flat on his back, Harvey looked up into her black eyes and showed a dry smile that was tinged with self-derision.

". . . I'm sorry you had to see me looking so pathetic," he murmured, his voice scratching at his parched throat.

Kieli shook her head lightly and smiled, "I'm glad." She seemed to be forcing a smile onto her troubled expression. Suddenly Harvey couldn't stand to see it and let out a sigh of unknown meaning. He ran both hands through his bangs and then left his arms over his face for a while.

"*What are you beating yourself up for* now?" came the radio's exasperated voice over the rock music. "Well, excuse me," he grumbled halfheartedly. Through his arms, he could see Kieli still gazing at him with that stiff expression. Seeing him and the Corporal like that must have shaken her up pretty badly, but even so, she hung in there and dragged them out of there. "Oh, I'm fine now."

He reached a hand out to touch Kieli's cheek, but Kieli started and pulled back slightly. It was only for an instant, but he got the feeling she had avoided him. When he automatically stopped his hand, Kieli looked surprised at herself, as if she hadn't done it on purpose, and said, "Oh, I'm sorry. I didn't mean to . . ."

"No," he interrupted her shortly and pulled his hand back. He erased his expression and looked up at his palm. He felt he could see the blood of the hundreds of people he had killed covering it and convinced himself that it was better that he hadn't dirtied her clean, white skin.

That was when he felt a faint vibration under his back.

Something was coming near them along the train track. He gasped and jumped up, but, still a little dizzy, he ended up putting his hand on the ground for support.

"Harve —"

"I'm fine. Don't touch me."

Still on one knee, he waved Kieli behind him and kept a

watchful eye on the track. Something was approaching from the direction opposite the tunnel — from their destination, the abandoned mine. It wasn't a train. It wasn't going fast enough, and it was smaller.

An old, dark gray cart finally came into view from beyond the darkness. The single, box-shaped car with no roof ran quickly along the tracks. He thought it was like the ghost train they had seen in the tunnel, but this was definitely a real cart.

He couldn't determine how best to react, and froze in place for the time being. The cart came to an abrupt stop in front of the platform.

There was no one inside.

". . . . . . ?" He furrowed his brow.

Kieli stuck her face out from behind him and whispered, "Someone's riding it."

When he looked, a dim, round light appeared above the cart, and a tin lantern with a triangular top faded into view, with the light at its center. The spirit of an old man dressed in rags emerged, seeping in from the darkness, holding the lantern in one hand.

The old man glanced at them from underneath his deep hood and slowly moved the lantern sideways. He seemed to be saying, "Get in."

She saw a tower rising blackly toward the night sky. It was a winch tower for pulling up the fossil resources mined from under the ground, and apparently it was the base where the miners started digging their tunnels deep into the earth. The cart reached the last straight stretch of railroad before its final destination and slid along the track.

Kieli sat on the cold floor of the empty, square cart and looked up at the tower ahead of them. Darkness enveloped the area, but the strange light that their old greeter carried ensured them a dim field of vision.

Harvey leaned against the opposite wall and threw his gaze in no particular direction. The color had returned to his face, but he still looked a little weary.

While they waited at the old station, the Corporal told her that Harvey's Undying "core" had probably resonated with the magnetic field in the tunnel and caused a spasm. He said that the ultrapure energy material that made up the Undyings' power sources was excavated from layers of the earth with the same qualities as that tunnel. Before the War, similar strata existed everywhere, supporting their advanced energy culture.

". . . I wonder what those are."

To the right and left of the track ahead of them, she could see a lot of sticklike things standing out of the ground. She leaned forward and strained her eyes in the darkness. *"Oooohhh . . ."* A low, roaring moan came from the radio hanging around her neck.

"I'm back. I'm back . . . !"

They were grave markers. Countless grave markers, standing in the wilderness.

Not one of them was a proper tombstone — iron rods with scraps of cloth tied to them, swords and rifles that would no longer be of any use. The sea of crude grave markers stretched endlessly across the black wilderness, telling how many people had died there and how cruel their deaths had been.

Grave markers surrounded the track as their spirit greeter (probably something like a grave keeper) guided the cart along at an unchanging speed.

Sometimes, one or two soldiers' spirits would rise above the grave markers and watch them go, looking as if they wanted to say something. "This place is suffocating . . ." Harvey sank down along the wall, as if hiding; he thrust a hand into his hair and hung his head.

Kieli dropped her gaze, unable to say anything.

Harvey killed at least a few of these people. He might have killed a few dozen of them, or lots more. And if the tunnel battle she dreamed about earlier was from the Corporal's memory, that would mean that Harvey was also the one to kill the Corporal. A Demon of War who had slaughtered as much as anyone could slaughter in the old War — just as the legends said — he had not hesitated to take the lives of many, wearing that empty expression on his face.

They arrived at a spot very close to the winch tower, and the cart stopped with a small clatter. Slowly, the grave keeper raised his lantern and pointed into the sea of grave markers.

She looked questioningly at Harvey. He didn't appear to want to get too close to the burial ground, but he nodded and stood up. He straddled the cart's side wall and got down onto the tracks, then turned around and held a hand out to her. But he seemed to realize something and quickly dropped it, looked away, and walked on ahead.

"Ah . . ." Kieli stood there for a second, then climbed up the wall and jumped down onto the tracks. The radio floated up lightly, then bounced onto her stomach.

The grave keeper floated through the cart and guided them swiftly along, lighting their feet with his lantern. Eventually, he stopped in front of one grave.

The grave marker he had led them to was a terribly crude one — only a rusty, weathering rifle with a cloth tied around it — but Kieli got the feeling that the crudeness was symbolic of the graves here. On the scrap, by now almost indiscernible as a piece of cloth, were sewn two small stars.

Black static spewed out of the radio and gathered to form the one-legged soldier. He took a step forward on his good leg and looked quietly down at the grave.

It must have been the Corporal's grave.

The staticky spirit had only ever looked like a black shadow before, but now Kieli could make out a distinct human shape. The back of a dark green soldier's uniform, stained with blood, mud, and soot. The fabric was riddled with bullet holes, and only a few scraps of fabric were wrapped around the knee joint on his missing right leg.

Even when she saw such a terrifying ghost, no fear came over her. The face that peered from the hat hanging low over his eyes was angular, its expression somehow sarcastic — it fit the impression she got from his voice perfectly. Kieli could imagine the expressions on the Corporal's face inside the radio when he taught her history, when he talked about music, when he cursed at Harvey — it actually made her a little happy to see it.

The Corporal stood silent in front of his own grave for a while, then turned around to face Kieli and Harvey.

"Thank you for taking me all this way, Herbie." His voice still came from Kieli's radio. She was used to hearing the staticky voice, and it felt pleasant to her ears. It was rough but warm.

"I can't accept your thanks. I'm the one who . . ."

"Herbie," the voice from the radio interrupted Harvey in a soft tone, *"that was war. It's only natural that we'd kill each other. That's all there is to it, right?"*

Harvey wiped the expression off his face and looked back at the Corporal, but eventually he smiled bitterly, closed his eyes, and muttered something under his breath. She thought he said, "Thanks."

Then the Corporal turned to Kieli. *"Well, then. This is good-bye, Kieli. Thanks to you, the last part of the trip was a fun one."*

"Yeah. I had fun, too," Kieli answered with a smile. That much, she was prepared to say. She had thought about a few other things, like, "I guess it'd be weird to say, 'Take care,'" and "It would be bad luck to say, 'Let's see each other again.'" But her plan was to just keep smiling and say, "Good-bye, Corporal."

But the words she had ready all flew out of her head, and completely different ones came to her mouth. "Don't go."

As she watched, the Corporal went speechless. Next to her, Harvey asked in surprise, "Kieli?" But now that she had started, the barrier she had built in her mind shattered, and the things that she had planned not to say came flooding out, one after another.

"Can't you stay in the radio forever? Then I can keep it, and we can be always be together. We just got to know each other; I don't want you to go. I don't want you to go!"

"Kieli . . ."

"What's with the tantrum all of a sudden? This isn't like you."

"It's *not* not like me! I was thinking it the whole time; I just wasn't saying it!" she yelled back at Harvey's questioning tone in spite of herself. She knew that saying it would only bother the Corporal and exasperate Harvey, but she couldn't stop. "I mean, I don't have Becca anymore; I'll be all alone again. The only people I can make friends with are dead, but they all leave me and go far away. I wish I was dead, too. I wish I was a ghost."

"Hey, that's not funny."

"I'm not trying to be funny. Should I die and become a ghost, too? Then can we be together forever?"

"Hey, cut it out!" he reprimanded her sharply, roughly grabbing her shoulders. She faltered a little under Harvey's stern expression, but she refused to back down, and instead rounded on him: "What do you care, Harvey? You're just going to go away somewhere, too!

"Kill me! Make me a ghost and take me with you! It would be easy for you, wouldn't it, Harvey!? Just like you did to the Corporal, kill —"

"*Kieli!*" The Corporal's angry shout flew from the radio and hit her in the abdomen. She stopped her rant with a gasp. *What did I just say?*

She looked up to see copper-colored eyes looking down at her, having lost their expression.

"I'm sorry, I didn't mean . . ."

I didn't mean to say those things. Her excuse stuck in her throat and never made it to her lips. The person in her mind who had been spurring her on to say those things had suddenly run away, and all at once her head cooled and her reason returned.

". . . I'm sorry, Harvey. I'm sorry . . ." She looked down, unable to face him; all she could do anymore was apologize. She hated herself. It wasn't their idea for her to tag along with them, and now she bothered them with this. Then to top it off, she said all those terrible things.

The tears that now overflowed from her eyes stained the ground here and there. On this weighty land, thick with the blood of soldiers, Kieli's tears were so light, so trivial; they were worth nothing. Standing in the middle of the graveyard, her own sobs were all that she could hear, unusually clear in the enveloping silence.

"Kieli." After a time, Harvey's quiet, emotionless voice came to her from overhead. "When we get back to town tomorrow, go back to Easterbury. I'll take you as far as the station."

Kieli hung her head, staring at the tips of Harvey's shoes, and didn't answer. Her chest hurt from trying too hard to control her sobbing. "Kieli," Harvey said again. His flat tone indicated that he was only reiterating, not giving her a choice in the matter. Kieli took a moment, then gave a small nod.

Harvey exhaled some cigarette smoke that rose into the dark gray sky, then gradually melted away and disappeared. The grave markers resembled dead branches as they extended in rows to the distant horizon; under the faintly brightening sky, he could tell that the cemetery in the wilderness was far more vast than they had seen in the darkness the night before.

Countless men had lost their lives here. And he had taken some — possibly a large number — of them himself.

As he leaned against the cart's outside wall, smoking and waiting for morning to arrive, he felt someone's presence next to him. The next thing he knew, the spirit of a soldier was standing beside him, gazing, like him, at the endless sea of graves.

"You going, Corporal?"

"Yeah. I'm thinking I'll leave before Kieli wakes up."

"I see." Harvey glanced behind him. The black-haired girl was sleeping soundly on the cart's floor, covering herself with her coat. Her face showed how long she had been crying; the Corporal's hushed voice came from the radio she held closely to her chest.

They wouldn't be able to start back until morning anyway, so the Corporal stayed one last night with Kieli. That night was about to end.

"Herbie, are you sure about this?"

"*Harve*y." He figured this would be the last time they had this exchange as he answered the Corporal, keeping his voice low so not to wake Kieli. "Sure about what?"

"Are you sure you're okay with leaving Kieli?"

"It doesn't matter if I'm okay with it. She just has a bit of a strong spiritual sense; other than that, she's a normal girl. She'll be happier living in normal society. If she's with me, she'll be living like an outcast."

"You can cut the act. What I'm asking is are you okay with it?"

"What's it got to do with me?" Harvey blinked. But the Corporal's gaunt profile only gazed at the grave markers in front of him and didn't answer. Taken aback, Harvey stared at the profile for a few seconds, then looked wordlessly back at the tombs. After inhaling a puff of smoke and exhaling it slowly, he responded, "I don't care. It's easier to be alone." After all the time he took to come up with a response, he could still only give a noncommittal one.

"You're more stubborn than I thought. For all the long time you've lived, it looks like the inside of your head hasn't matured much."

"Well, excuse me."

He thought he saw the Corporal smirk, but his shape gradually faded and he could no longer make out an expression. The sand-colored morning sun pierced a small gap in the thick clouds and began to illuminate the graveyard.

"One more thing, Herbie."

"*Harvey*. This really is the last time I'm gonna correct you."

The Corporal's appearance gradually disappeared, as if melting into the morning light. *"The truth is you wanted to die here, isn't it? You ending up agreeing to bring me here, and visiting your old friends — it looked to me like you were squaring off past accounts. . . ."*

The voice from the radio dissolved into the silence with his form, and those became the last words of the spirit that had possessed the radio.

Harvey stared at the empty space where the soldier's spirit had been for a while after that. He noticed ash from his cigarette falling onto his shoe and looked down at it, then closed his eyes and let out a bitter laugh. *You didn't have to worry about me in your last moments. . . .*

". . . Well, I guess we'd better set out soon, too."

He had to wake Kieli, but when he thought of the look on her face when she opened her eyes to find out that the Corporal was no longer inside the radio, he faltered. He heaved a sigh and dropped his cigarette butt onto the track. As he was about to stamp it out, he let out an involuntarily yelp as he suddenly lost his support and tottered backward.

When he turned around, the cart was running. "Just a . . . What?" Panicking, he rushed after it and grabbed its side wall; it sped up all at once the instant he jumped inside and slid down the track. The grave-keeper ghost had suddenly appeared above the cart, driving it straight for the abandoned mine's winch tower, sometimes throwing worried glances behind them.

"What the . . . ?" When Harvey leaned over the cart's back wall and squinted at the far end of the train tracks, he could see the headlights of a train far off in the brightening wilderness. It must have been a big train; he could feel its vibrations coming through the tracks.

"Harvey? What?" a girl's nervous voice came from behind him. The cart's movement had woken her up, and Kieli sat on the floor and looked to either side in bewilderment, holding her coat and the radio. He glanced back to confirm, then threw his gaze back to their rear.

It was a blackened train, covered in excessive armor. It quickly closed the gap between them and appeared as if it would flatten the small cart.

He turned around to see the impending winch tower waiting in front of them, its arched mouth open wide. The instant the cart slipped inside, the outside scene changed completely, as if a curtain had dropped, to an enclosed, indoor scene.

"It's an armored Church car," Harvey said quickly, turning on his heels and crouching in front of Kieli. "If you scream, you'll bite your tongue. Got it?"

He didn't wait for an answer, but wrapped his arm around her waist and picked her up, using his other arm as a pivot to jump over the wall and throw himself out of the cart. "Hya!" Kieli started to scream, but swallowed it back as Harvey had told her. At the same time he landed, he made a 180-degree turn, the lower half of Kieli's body flailing, and braked by scraping his knee and shoe against the ground. Smoke hissed from his sole.

Immediately afterward, the train charged into the tunnel with a thunderous roar and smashed the cart to smithereens. The grave-keeper ghost left behind a feeble scream, resembling a ringing in the ears, as it vanished. Kieli, clinging to Harvey's neck, let out an astonished cry in his ear.

The armored train stopped, half of its body of linked black cars inside the tunnel. Clouds of smoke billowed from its wheels, and before they dissipated, doors opened in the train's sides, revealing people (assuming they were humans inside) wearing full-faced white armor. Every one of them carried a weighty, high-caliber gun in his arms. They were uniquely stocky guns, somewhat shorter than rifles, with thicker barrels.

Carbonization guns . . .

They were the special guns of the Church Soldiers' Undying hunters. Harvey swore under his breath. Assuming he was right, and they were after him, where did they find him out?

He cursed himself for getting too comfortable after so many years of boredom.

He rapidly scanned the area around him, looking for a place to escape, as he backed away from them. The only exit to the outside was blocked by the enormous armored train. He could see that a lift went deep under the winch tower, but not whether it was broken or was at a lower level. There was no lift at the landing, just a square shaft gaping open on the other side of the rails closing it off.

Guess I'll have to jump . . .

He would have avoided that option if he could have, but at the moment he couldn't come up with any better ideas, so he turned on his heels, still holding Kieli. He could manage it by himself, but he wasn't confident that he could keep Kieli safe, jumping when he didn't know how far down it was or what it was like at the bottom.

It was then that he saw, out of the corner of his eye, the front line of Church Soldiers readying their strangely shaped carbonization guns.

"Get away!" he said, shaking the girl off his neck and pushing her away, and then . . .

Fwa-boom!

The sound unique to the firing of a carbonization gun rang through to the winch tower's ceiling. Four shots rang out in succession. He felt the shock of the first bullet as it blew a chunk out of his right leg; the rest merely bored into the ground at his feet.

"Kuh!" He automatically put out his right leg to steady himself, but, having no support, the leg collapsed onto the ground; he lost his balance and toppled over.

"Harvey!"

"Idiot! I said stay away!" He pushed Kieli aside as she

ran to him and tried to shield him. The Church Soldiers' second attack —

The second attack didn't come. For some reason, the Church Soldiers held their fire, as if unsure how to react.

". . . . . ?"

Harvey fixed his gaze on the enemy and thought for a second, then wrapped his arm around Kieli's neck. A few of them raised their guns instinctively. "Wait!" The one who seemed to be their leader restrained them. *Of course. . . .*

"Don't move!" Harvey's voice echoed against the tower's high ceiling, surprising Kieli, and she stopped moving. And for some reason, the Church Soldiers, aiming their guns this way, froze as well.

Then Harvey's arms grabbed her from behind, lifting her up and covering her mouth so violently his fingers dug into her cheek. "Make a move, and I break her neck," Harvey said, in a menacing voice, and, still holding Kieli, he backed away slowly, with one arm and one leg.

She didn't really understand the situation. Harvey had captured her and was covering her mouth. He was saying that if they moved, he would break "her" neck — probably Kieli's. The Church Soldiers didn't move.

"Kieli. Be quiet and do what I tell you. Understand?" Harvey whispered into the confused Kieli's ear, in a tone that only Kieli would hear. When she gave a small nod, her mouth still covered, Harvey loosened his grip some.

"They're only after me. You were only tricked. You didn't know I'm an Undying. They're going to help you and take you into protective custody. If they ask you about me, you just have to tell them you don't know anything. They'll believe you. Because it doesn't make any sense that a girl from boarding school would be with an Undying. You can go back to the boarding school and go back to your normal life without being suspected of anything."

"No," Kieli replied immediately, shaking her head slightly. Harvey tightened his grip around her neck. "But what will you do, Harvey? Will I ever see you again?" she asked, clinging to his arm and looking up at him.

". . . I'll run," was the only response he gave. He didn't answer her second question.

Harvey retreated as far as the lift's landing and stopped. All too ready to spring into action, one man in armor stepped forward, but another armored hand held him back — because Harvey squeezed his "hostage's" neck. His fingers dug mercilessly into the nape of her neck, choking her, and Kieli let out a hoarse scream.

"Harve . . ."

"I'm sorry. I have to show them I mean it," he whispered in her ear, in a cold, comfortless voice. "This is perfect; they saved me the trouble of taking you to the station. Relax. They'll take you back and treat you all right."

As he groped behind him for the lift's iron railing, Harvey stood up, dragging Kieli with him, then tottered on his foot. "Harvey, no. I mean, you're hurt . . ." Kieli spoke up impulsively, but he covered her mouth again.

". . . Good-bye, Kieli. You'll never see me again." With that final remark, he let go of Kieli's neck and shoved her in the back. Kieli slouched forward, stumbled, and fell to the ground.

The Church Soldiers took that as a signal and made their move in unison. Harvey turned on his heels and jumped over the rail. Concentrated fire flew over Kieli's head into the elevator landing as she lay flat on her face.

By that time, Harvey had disappeared into the shaft.

"Raise the lift!" a muffled voice yelled angrily through its owner's helmet, and the metallic footsteps of the men in armor chased hurriedly after him.

Kieli didn't have the energy to stand. One of the armored men knelt beside her and said something to make sure she was safe, but his voice and the commotion around them all sounded so far away and didn't penetrate into her head. The last thing Harvey said, his low voice and breathing as he whispered in her ear, the subtle intonation of every single word, echoed in the core of her brain. *Good-bye, Kieli. You'll never see me again. Good-bye, Kieli. . . .*

"We blew a chunk out of his leg. He can't have gone far. Find him," a determined shout passed over his head, followed by the sound of lots of footsteps. Wrinkling his brow at the thought that it was a Church Soldier, supposedly a pure, upright servant of God saying those things, Harvey waited until the footstops had gone a long way away and crawled out of a cavity in the earth.

The tunnel continued beyond the darkness, surrounded by imposing rock walls on three sides. A narrow track for mine carts ran along the ground, but it was broken in places and wouldn't be of any use.

"Damn . . ." He started to walk with only his left leg, dragging his right leg and using the rock wall for support. They'd completely taken off the muscle and bone from below his knee to his ankle, and his right foot could only dangle — it had been rendered completely useless for actions such as walking. Not a single drop of blood fell from the black, carbonized wound.

The abnormal regeneration speed of an Undying's cells existed in their unique blood; using that knowledge, the Undying Hunters carried guns that not only reduced a wide target area to ash, but evaporated the Undyings' blood. To reactivate their healing ability, they would have no choice but to use a blade or something to deepen a wound further to get it to bleed. It ended up in a very masochistic situation that no sane person would be able to handle; and on top of that, they would have to wait for the newly carved wound to heal, so it could hardly be called efficient.

"I'm such an idiot . . ." Harvey cursed at himself as he walked. He meant to concentrate all his energies on moving himself forward, but one half of his brain was thinking of something else.

He shouldn't have taken Kieli with him to begin with — he'd put her in danger and ended up giving her to the Church, of all things, and to put it bluntly, he couldn't help any of that now. But the betrayed look on her face when he told her she would never see him again — that one thing burned into his eyes and would not leave. He didn't think having her look at him like that would affect him so much.

Argh, I'm such an idiot . . .

Ahead of him, things got noisy again, and he could see the flickers of returning lights. He ran his eyes to the right and left and found an inconspicuous hollow in the wall next to him that led to a side tunnel. An iron railing closed it off. It was impossible for him to climb over it, so he crawled through the opening underneath. He had just managed, somehow, to pull his entire body through with his arms when the footsteps came back. He plastered himself to the wall and held his breath. About half of the men who had gone deeper into the tunnel ran past on the path he had just taken.

He breathed a sigh of relief for the time being and set his sights farther down the side tunnel. He got the feeling it was faintly brighter, and he started in that direction, leaning against the wall.

Light from the morning sky leaked in through the ceiling of the tunnel ahead. It wasn't low enough for him to climb, although if his leg weren't in such bad shape, he might have been able to scale it anyway. A wire hung down from overhead and connected to a simple lift that carried things up and down. It was the type with two platforms that went up and down alternately — one was overhead, the other down below.

Will it move . . . ?

He didn't expect it to move, but if worse came to worst, if the wire would at least hold, it probably wouldn't be impossible for him to climb up it. Grasping at this faint hope, he quickened his pace, dragging his foot. Just then, he heard a small clatter behind him.

"Ephraim," someone called in a muffled voice. Before he could decide whether to turn around or not, a gunshot rang out; a blast hit his right shoulder, sending him flying backward. All at once, he jabbed his nails into the wall and planted his feet, scratching the wall as he saved himself from falling over.

An armored Church Soldier stood under the poor light from the side tunnel. For now, it looked as if there was only one of them. He shook the carbonization gun he supported in both hands; the empty cartridge clattered onto the ground as he loaded the next round.

Harvey didn't wait; he kicked the ground with his left foot. If his right foot had been functional, he would have used it as a pivot and attacked, but in his current state, all he could do was deliver a suicide tackle. He used the force from the tackle to jam his elbow into a break in the armor. A sound of breaking bones came from his opponent's ribs, and possibly also from his own elbow.

They fell in a jumbled heap on the ground. He got up, picked up the carbonization gun that had flown from his opponent's hands, and pulled the trigger. A dull gunshot sounded and the recoil threw him back into the wall; small rocks rained down on his head.

Black smoke rose from his opponent's carbonized abdomen, and the man stopped moving. His armor had probably absorbed the impact to some degree, but the shot was made at point-blank range.

Sitting against the wall, still holding the gun, Harvey stiffened and stared for a while at the dead body lying on the ground.

"Aaaaugh . . ." he let out a long, deep sigh. He may have been the one in danger, but there was no need to be so quick to blow out the middle of the guy's body. The moment his ribs were shattered, he wouldn't have been able to move anymore. But Harvey's body moved automatically, and the next thing he knew, he had killed him.

He had tried so hard not to kill anyone, and if they'd just left him alone, he wouldn't have, so why did they have to keep coming after him?

"I have to hurry . . ." he muttered, sighing again. He dropped the carbonization gun that weighed so heavily in his arms onto the ground. The other soldiers would most likely come running at the sound of that gunshot.

He tried to stand up and realized that he couldn't really do that anymore. After his right shoulder took that hit, his right arm was still attached, more or less, but he couldn't lift it. It was difficult to stand with only one arm and one leg.

He had no choice but to crawl along the ground toward the lift. He swept the fear that it wouldn't move out of his mind, along with the idea that, in his condition, there was no way he could do anything as spectacular as climbing that wire. But there was light from outside there — it was a dim light, hidden in sand-colored clouds; but the color of the earth and sky that had cherished the planet's scarcely remaining resources, storing them in their bosom, poured down in a sparkling ray. And anyway, he had the vague idea that if he could get under that light, everything would be okay.

Clinging to the ground with only a left arm, he used everything he had to pull himself forward. Blood oozed under his fingernails as they peeled off when he scratched the hard ground.

Why am I trying so desperately to get away? he suddenly questioned himself. He was in a similar situation eighty years ago. When he reached the battlefield wilderness, lined with corpses, he got tired of it all and stopped going on. He could just stop now, like he did then. This time, the Church Soldiers would have no trouble finding him and doing him the favor of killing him.

He stopped putting his arm forward. He lifted his head and looked up at the light ahead for a while.

As he dimly thought something along the lines of how the modest softness of that sand-colored light was a lot like the atmosphere that surrounded Kieli, he murmured in a whisper, "I guess I can go a little further . . . ," and started dragging himself forward again after all.

He reached the shaft through which the light penetrated. He crawled onto the lift's bottom plank, stretched his arm out from an impossible position, and grabbed the operating lever. He pulled it down a little, and it responded; the wire went taut. Miraculously, it looked like it would move.

If I make it out of here, I guess I can go see her face just once. Even just watching her from a distance to see that she's doing okay. He dwelled on these thoughts that, for him, sounded extremely attached to life, and this time, he put some energy into pulling the lever. "— !"

He turned around instinctively, automatically, as if someone had grabbed his cheeks and forced him.

The armored Church Soldier stood up slowly and picked up the fallen carbonization gun, his abdomen still smoking. A piece of his cracked mask had fallen off, revealing the soldier's face underneath.

Suddenly, he remembered. It was only in the space of an instant, but he had called him by his old name.

"Hey there, Ephraim. So it's been eighty years, has it?" the Church Soldier said, twisting the ends of his mouth into a crescent. The blue-gray eyes that showed a hint of madness, the thin lips forming a twisted smile. He was a man with a strange presence, having no other characteristics but those eyes that left any impression, and that fact in itself left an impression.

"Joachim? Why are you . . . ?" Harvey muttered the name of his old comrade (although he didn't want to call him a comrade) in astonishment, still in the posture he was in when he crawled up onto the lift. Smiling as if Harvey's surprise amused him, the soldier swung the awkward gun up and reloaded. His smile was as depressing and annoying as ever.

"Actually, the Church hired me to collect 'cores.' Right now, even your heart would fetch a price so high I could buy a continent with it."

"Never mind that you're an Undying yourself . . ."

"Oh, but that's exactly why I have to do my job — my own life would be in danger otherwise. Really, I'd rather sit back and talk about old times."

"I don't want to talk to you for even a second," he spat, literally, interrupting the soldier's depressing and annoying small talk.

The soldier's composed smile changed completely, twisting in displeasure. "Then shut up."

Without the slightest hesitation, he pulled the trigger.

Give me a break. Here the grave keeper calls me, so I come back to see what's up and find this. I can't even disappear in peace.

Floating in the air over the coal mine, a soldier looked down at the corpse lying at the bottom of the narrow shaft.

It wasn't as if he wasn't vaguely interested in seeing how the Undying die. The young man lay faceup on the lift's lower platform, the center of his body blown out by impact from a bullet. As he looked down on his copper-colored eyes, they seemed to be glaring up at him, but there was no longer any light in them.

He was in terrible shape — he'd lost half the use of the right side of his body — but that wouldn't be enough to stop an Undying's life functions. There was a hole gouged unceremoniously in the center of his chest where his core, his heart, should have been buried. The bio-cables that had connected his core to the inside of his body had been torn apart, and thick blood resembling coal tar oozed out of them.

That's how the young man had expired.

The soldier sighed. Well, not like he had breath.

What are you gonna do? You could just end it right here. That is what you wanted, right?

The youth didn't answer, only pierced the air with his empty gaze. Apparently when they, these unnatural beings, died, they didn't become ghosts like he did. It was said that they lived for eternity, but they seemed like such fragile, fleeting, short-lived creatures.

What will you do, Herbie? If you feel like living a little longer, you wanna put some effort into it?

CHAPTER 6

HOW MANY MORE STEPS TO
THE LIGHT MARKING THE WAY?

It wasn't as if there were any clear-cut boundaries between the seasons, but the day after the Colonization Days break, the air took on a definite winter feel, with no room for a single bit of autumn to sneak in.

"Finished."

Kieli gave the mound of earth a light pat with both hands and paused for breath. Rubbing her fingers together after the cold outside air and digging in the ground had thoroughly frozen them, she turned to look beside her.

"I'm sorry it's not very good."

An emaciated black cat sat next to Kieli as she crouched on the ground. It didn't react to her voice; it only stared at the little mountain of earth in front of it. Its gray eyes matched the winter sky; she couldn't read whether they were exasperated or angry, or maybe happy.

Kieli faced forward again and, side by side with the black cat, looked down at the ground at her feet. There was a humble grave in a corner of the courtyard, made simply by digging a shallow hole and refilling it with earth. Hugging her knees, she closed her eyes for a brief moment and offered a prayer for the small life.

"Kieli, what are you slacking off around here for? Are you trying to make me do all the cleaning?" a sharp voice snapped behind her. Still squatting, she turned around to see her freckled classmate standing in the school passage. She was pushing a cart piled high with thick books.

When she saw her, Kieli remembered that, oh yeah, school was over for the day. She wiped her dirty hands on her skirt and stood up. She didn't see any reason to hurry, so she walked at a normal pace (though, thanks to a certain somebody, she got the feeling her normal pace had quickened quite a bit) back to the outside hallway. When she got there, Zilla, who had been waiting in total annoyance, glanced at the courtyard and asked, "What is that?"

"A cat. It was dead," Kieli answered in short sentences as she took over pushing the cart.

She found the cat frozen to death in the shadows of the hall this morning, on her way back to class after the combination winter term opening ceremonies and morning worship service in the auditorium. She skipped her afternoon classes, found a little spade in the shed, and buried it in a corner of the courtyard where no one would step on it.

Zilla looked cynically at the tiny grave, then took on a somewhat joking tone and snickered. "Don't tell me it was a cat you used to summon a demon?"

Kieli didn't change her expression; she only glanced sideways at her classmate and started pushing the cart toward the building on the other side of the hall.

"What? Talk back. You're no fun!" Temporarily left behind, Zilla complained selfishly and went after Kieli. Kieli thought, *Oh so she* wanted *me to talk back*, but she didn't feel like responding and so kept pushing the cart in silence.

Just then, she felt something coil around her feet. When she looked down, the black cat rubbed against her legs and meowed. After that, it circled once around Kieli and disappeared.

"Did you hear something?"

As Zilla looked around suspiciously, Kieli gave a vague, "Hmm," and smiled to herself as she looked down at the cart and kept walking. *So he liked it? I'm glad.*

She got the feeling this was the first time in days that she had smiled a little. But she had shed all her emotions since the incident at the mine. It had gotten to be a pain to converse with people, so she only spoke in broken sentences.

The soldiers brought her back to the boarding school on the last day of the Colonization Days holiday.

The headmistress and Miss Hanni had already heard the story that an Undying had tricked her and taken her to the abandoned mine, and the Church Soldiers had rescued her just as he was about to eat her head first; Kieli didn't know what explanation she had been given, but apparently that's how Miss Hanni understood it. She greeted Kieli with an embrace, accompanied by her self-intoxicated laments and overreactions, as a pitiable student who had gone through a terrifying experience that must have scarred her emotionally. She wished it had been the Church history teacher who greeted her. *It must have been awful, Kieli. Of course you don't have to write a report.*

But instead, Miss Hanni told her that she needed to forget those sinful, sinful memories of associating with an Undying as soon as possible, so she was to keep the incident a secret, of course from the other students, but also from the other teachers. Her Church history teacher remained ignorant of the reason she hadn't been able to write a report, so on her first day of the winter term, Kieli was forced to stand in the hall for an hour, only to be released after receiving an oh-so-generous three-day extension to write twice as long a report. Like she could write twice as much in three days.

Kieli yawned and looked up at the clock on her writing desk; it was almost time for the date to change.

She put her pen down on the report paper, which remained blank even after several hours, and breathed a little sigh. She noticed that the lazy idea of going to bed was about to overcome her, and suddenly became aware of the reality that her daily routine had returned.

In comparison to the few days of her trip, with each day packed full of events, she spent her life at the boarding school by leaving everything to momentum, with no major differences between today and tomorrow — no, her daily routine hadn't returned. When she got back, there was something missing from that routine.

"Becca, I'm going to bed," she said tentatively, as she cleaned up her desk like she did every day, turning to look at the beds against the wall, like she did every day, and addressing her roommate, like she did every day.

Good night, Kieli.

The bright soprano voice no longer answered. The lower of the metal bunk beds was arranged with Kieli's bedding about halfway complete; the top bunk was empty, and dust lay thick on the flattened mattress. The selfish, free-spirited roomate who would lie there pretending to read a book and sometimes talk to Kieli, demanding a reaction to everything, heedless of the fact that Kieli was trying to do her homework, was no longer there.

The double room that she lived in by herself was strangely big and empty.

"......"

She froze for a while with her head still turned toward the bed, then slowly brought her downcast gaze back to her desk. Her eyes stopped on the old radio she had placed on the corner of her desk. It was dented in places, its coating had almost completely peeled off, and there were signs that the speaker had been torn and reattached many times. She reached out, pulled it closer, and turned it on. After a smart little burst of static, music flowed from the speakers at a low volume and filled the room.

Since Kieli had first met the radio, it had always been set to the same frequency — not a legitimate channel, but a guerrilla one, known only to those who knew to look for it. It was possible that the tuner itself was broken. But she was afraid of losing the faint waves from this channel, so she didn't even think of experimenting with it.

She wondered who had first turned it to this frequency. She had no trouble imagining a red-haired man sitting cross-legged on the seat of a train, adjusting the tuner as the voice from the radio urged him on. *Just a little higher, higher; argh, you went too far, you moron. I told you just a little, Herbie.*

The radio only carried melodies from some far-off place now; it would no longer talk to her in its low, staticky voice, in its rough but kind tone. And she would never again look at those long fingers that turned the tuner from the seat diagonally across as they lit a cigarette, moving in slight annoyance at the effort involved; and those hands would never again reach out to her.

She wondered why she had been afraid, even for an instant, and avoided that hand that tried to touch her cheek at the abandoned station, and her mind filled with thoughts she would never regret enough. Even though she was painfully aware that Harvey blamed himself more than anyone. Even though she knew that that big, warm hand that held hers at the carnival didn't exist for the sake of war anymore.

She pursed her lips and pushed back the feelings that welled up inside her.

She was sure Harvey had escaped safely and would be looking out over the Sand Ocean in the far east as if he was tired of it about now. *When he hears the "all aboard," he'll stoop down to pick up his bag, and walk over to the boat landing at his usual fast pace — if only he would look back and call out to me. "I'm gonna leave you behind, Kieli. What are you doing? Is the ocean that unusual?"*

"No, don't think about it . . ." she muttered, exhausted, and dropped her head onto the desk. She pressed her forehead against the radio; its cold touch cooled her temples and somehow she managed to hold back her tears.

My short journey is over. *Good-bye, Kieli. You'll never see me again. . . .*

In the end, it turned out that Kieli would never have to write her report.

She had fallen asleep in that position the previous night, and when she woke up in the morning, red marks from the radio clearly showed on half of her face, so she had just decided to independently cancel her lectures when Miss Hanni summoned her. She didn't know if it was because she had skipped her afternoon classes the day before, or if they had somehow discovered her attempt to be absent today, but anyway, she was sure that if they were taking her to the headmistress's office this early in the morning, it must be that she could no longer receive financial aid and they were kicking her out of the school. These were the thoughts that filled her head as she followed Miss Hanni through the door to the headmistress's office. She completely forgot to be polite and say "excuse me."

The headmistress sat at the desk in the very back. She was a middle-aged woman who wore the long black robes of the clergy; Kieli didn't have any significant memories of her.

There was one more person sitting in the room on the guest couch in front of the desk — a young man who wore the robes of a priest on pilgrimage.

"Hey there, Kieli. I'm glad I could see you again."

The priest rose with a gentle manner from the sofa and stood in front of Kieli. Kieli gaped up at him as the headmistress's cheerful voice addressed her from behind him, "This is Mr. Joachim, from the capital. He says you've met before?"

The sentence did not jog her memory; she lifted her chin and scrutinized the tall man, with no idea of who he was. He looked down at her from the same eye level as a certain someone she had gotten used to looking up at during her vacation, and her heart skipped a beat. That was what finally reminded her. She didn't remember anything other than his blue-gray eyes and that he was about as tall as Harvey, but he was the priest she had met at the transfer station.

"Oh!" she breathed, sounding silly even to herself, then, "The capital?" The first half of what the headmistress had said only just now took her by surprise; her eyes widened and she looked back up at the priest. If he was a priest from the capital, didn't that mean he was a Church leader?

A mischievous smile lit the priest's gentle eyes. "Surprised?"

"Yes. You didn't seem like anyone that important at all." She nodded honestly, but apparently she was too honest, and, over the priest's shoulder, she saw the headmistress's smile freeze. "K-Kieli!" Miss Hanni's panicked whisper flew at her at an angle from behind.

"It's all right. She's still young." The priest put the two women at ease with his practiced response and looked back at Kieli. "Easterbury happened to be my last stop, so I thought I would drop by and thank you for the other day."

"You went to all that trouble?" It may have been some kind of fate, but they had only met for a few minutes in front of the station, and she didn't even remember his face. He probably figured out her school from her uniform, but she didn't think she'd done anything to merit his coming all this way to see her.

The priest didn't even blush at Kieli's question, and answered very straighforwardly, "Yes, I just had to see you one more time." He bent down and peered worriedly into her face. "I've been talking with the headmistress just now, and I understand you've had a terrible experience. Are you all right?"

The "terrible experience" her teachers had heard was that Kieli was almost eaten, and Kieli didn't have any such "terrible" memories, but when he asked if she was all right, she somehow got the feeling that he knew everything; he had taken her off guard and she started crying in spite of herself. Even though she hadn't shed a single tear since it happened.

". . . I'm fine . . ." That was all she managed to mutter as she stared at the floor; the next line wouldn't pass her lips. *I'm fine. Nobody did anything to me. If you care enough to ask me those questions, then please stop running him down.*

The headmistress and Miss Hanni fell silent at Kieli's sudden tears; and for a while, only Kieli's stifled sobs filled the headmistress's room. Eventually the headmistress deliberately cleared her throat and, "N-now, now. Let's not talk of such painful experiences," and tried to smooth everything over with a line that revealed her misunderstanding of the situation.

"Mr. Joachim has a wonderful proposition for you."

Kieli wiped her eyes on the sleeve of her uniform and looked up. In contrast to Kieli's dubious gaze, she could see in the headmistress's face a sense of absolute trust for this promising young priest from the capital. She plastered a broad, good-natured educator's smile on her face, that nevertheless left no deep impression on Kieli's mind, then nodded importantly and said, "He says he would like to invite you to the middle school division of the seminary in the capital on a scholarship," she informed her, clapping her hands together.

Kieli blinked, trying to take in what had just been said. She shifted her gaze to the priest, who responded with a smile and added, "I'm told you have no relatives, so, if you like, I was hoping you would come to the capital with me."

"But why me . . . ?"

"Oh, Kieli, isn't that marvelous!?" Miss Hanni raised her shrill voice before Kieli could ask her question. She looked up at the ceiling, clasped her hands in front of her chest, closed her eyes, and said rapturously, "This is guidance from the Lord. He gives equal opportunities even to unfortunate girls like you."

Kieli took her eyes off the priest and gazed expressionlessly at Miss Hanni's rimless glasses. She wanted to ask this believer who was so honest and virtuous that she would call this unfortunate girl "unfortunate" to her face, "Miss Hanni, if God really is here, then why didn't He give that black cat even a little food or shelter from the cold?"

Then she suddenly came up with something. Maybe God really was on their planet. And He was a man of such perfect, flawless character, that He watched over everyone equally — the strong and the weak, the rich and the poor — and never played favorites or reached His hand out to any of them. *Oh, what a wonderful God. He can just drop dead.*

The transfer station on the eastern edge of Easterbury parish was bustling with travelers as usual today. Railways stretched in different directions toward varying destinations — to the west, the railroad went through central Easterbury and on in the direction of Westerbury; to the east, lay the Sand Ocean that spanned the continent; and to the north, the railroad passed through the North-hairo parish and on to the Church Capital.

Kieli leaned her cheek on the cold glass of the train window and gazed indifferently at the people hurrying on and off the platforms, carrying their big bags.

She couldn't quite believe that only a week had passed since the last time she saw this scene. The last time, Kieli and her companions had gotten off here, visited Harvey's old house, and then headed for the abandoned railroad to the south.

It was possible that Harvey was still in the area, and that if she looked for him, she could see him. Never learning her lesson, she got her hopes up and started to fidget slightly; she made herself sick.

Just stop thinking about it already. Harvey said I'd never see him again. And now I'm going far away from here.

She had already boarded the train leaving for the capital and was waiting for departure.

Kieli didn't want to go on to attend a seminary, so she refused the scholarship, but of course that was when it was determined that her financial aid in Easterbury would be cut off. The headmistress and Miss Hanni had not a speck of doubt that Kieli would happily go, and in the end, she couldn't oppose her teachers' opinions.

She wanted to hurry and be able to make her own living and decide for herself where she was going to go. She had started vaguely thinking along those lines after experiencing her journey, but now she was in a position where she had no choice but to depend on financial aid and scholarships.

And one more thing — she couldn't completely refuse to go to the capital, because Kieli had no reason to be so set on staying in Easterbury. It wasn't like she had any family, and Becca was gone; besides, it wasn't like anyone would come to get her if she waited for them. . . .

Who was she thinking of?

I'm thinking about it again . . .

Just as she interrupted her own thoughts and sighed, a voice beside her said, "Here," and a tin mug was offered to her. White steam rose slowly from it, and a sweet-smelling brown liquid swirled inside. When she looked up and accepted it in both hands, the young priest smiled and sat in the seat opposite her, a cup with a blacker liquid than hers in his hand.

"Apparently it will be a while before we depart. Drink that while we wait."

Kieli put the warm chocolate to her mouth and tasted it a little. *What a luxury!* she thought. *They've never served anything like this in the boarding school cafeteria.* Then she turned her eyes upward to look at the priest and said, "I like it."

"If you like it, I can get you another."

"You're such a friendly and considerate person, Mr. Joachim." She spoke her mind openly.

Joachim put his coffee to his own mouth and blinked. "I wonder if you're comparing me to someone when you say that? Perhaps you know someone who is unfriendly and inconsiderate?"

"No, it's not that," Kieli answered vaguely and looked nowhere in particular, trying to escape his gaze. She wished he would sit more to the side. It made her strangely nervous to have him sit directly across and stare at her like that.

She took another sip from her cup and glanced back at him. He was still staring at her, and she had the feeling he was scrutinizing her for something, which made her even more uncomfortable. His smile seemed friendly at first glance, but — and maybe she was wrong — it also looked as if there was a kind of thin membrane over it, and it was difficult to tell what he was thinking.

Why would he be interested in someone like her? Inviting her to the capital just for helping him a little in front of the station was awfully nice.

At a loss for where to look, she dropped her eyes back down to the chocolate in her cup. Just then, the car shook forward and back with a clank, and she very nearly spilled her drink and stained her skirt. She didn't need her boarding school uniform anymore, but all her personal clothes were packed in her luggage, and she ended up wearing her usual black uniform anyway.

Looking at the platform, she could see that they were doing something to the front of the train. She squinted her eyes to see what it was. "Ah!" Kieli half rose out of her seat and stuck her face to the window.

They were trying, just now, to attach an angular black car to the front passenger car of the train. It looked exactly like the Church Soldiers' armored car that had attacked them in the abandoned mine — she was almost sure of it.

"Mr. Joachim, what are they doing?" she asked, still clinging to the window.

For his part, Joachim calmly drank his coffee, not particularly concerned. "It seems the locomotive is having trouble. Since the Church Soldiers that had been deployed in Easterbury were going back now anyway, it's been decided that the armored car will pull the passenger train to the capital with it. It will delay our departure a little, but that car has more power; it will make up for it in speed."

"Church Soldiers . . ." Kieli murmured in a tense voice, then stared at the work going on in front of them.

With the three black cars connected to the front, the ten passenger cars, and the two freight cars at the end for a total of fifteen, the train was getting to be extremely long. She spotted a few men wearing the white armor among the people working on the platform, and her heart started beating faster.

She was getting a bad feeling about all of this. Had Harvey really gotten away?

Just then, she heard the sound of metal against metal next to her seat; she started and turned around to see a man, in the same armor as the people outside, standing in the aisle. Kieli almost screamed in spite of herself; she somehow managed to swallow it back, but she staggered and her back crashed into the window.

Kieli could hardly hold herself up for the fear she felt. Right in front of her, the Church Soldier leaned toward Joachim and whispered something in his ear, then left along the aisle, his spurs clanking as he went.

Even after the footsteps disappeared behind the door to the next car, Kieli remained rigid against the window. She felt the color drain from her entire body. Church Soldiers and priests held places on opposite ends of the Church's organization and had different jurisdictions, so until now, Kieli never made a connection between the incident in the mine and Joachim. But when she thought about it, if he was a Church leader, it wouldn't be so strange for him to be receiving reports.

"I'll be in the car up ahead a little ways. I'll come back later," Joachim said, rising from his seat as if to follow the soldier. He turned his eyes on her pallid, frozen face, and said kindly, "What's the matter? There's nothing to worry about."

"Um . . ." Kieli managed to open her mouth, using every effort to keep her voice from shaking. "The Undying that was with me. Didn't he escape? Could it be that you caught him?" Her efforts were in vain, and the voice that came from her throat was faint and trembling.

"Oh, neither," Joachim answered, still smiling, and went into the aisle, leaving Kieli unable to understand his meaning. He went a little ways, then stopped, turned casually back, and with the same smile plastered on his face, but with his cheeks somehow twisted strangely, he added, "It's all right. He's dead."

Kieli opened her eyes, thinking that someone was calling her.

For a second, she didn't realize that she had been asleep. The train had already departed. Quiet music, almost drowned out by the noise inside the car, reached Kieli's ears. She pulled the radio out of her luggage and placed it on her lap.

It didn't look as if Joachim had come back after leaving his seat.

What did he say earlier? Dead? Undying don't die. That's stupid. You're lying.

For some reason, her body had no energy, as if her nerves were paralyzed somewhere. She threw an absentminded glance out the window, still leaning an ear toward the radio. She couldn't see the scenery outside because of the darkness that enveloped it, and instead, the black glass reflected her own face and the inside of the car, giving her a strange sense of realism, like she was looking at translucent spirits.

She felt as though someone called her again.

She moved her head a little and turned her eyes toward the aisle and the seats on the other side. Sitting in the next box were a small girl and a man who appeared to be her father; the father was engrossed in his book, and the girl was leaning on him, sleeping. At the moment, there were no signs of anyone walking down the aisle.

She tilted her head in confusion. When she returned her gaze to the window, she heard, "... *li* ..."

This time there was no doubt about it — someone had called her. She looked around her again, then gasped, picked the radio up from her lap, and put her ear to the speaker. "*Ki* ... *li* ..." She heard a staticky voice call her name, so faint it almost vanished, but definitely there.

"Corp —" Kieli cried involuntarily, her voice hysterical, and stood up. On the other side of her box's partitions, the other passengers bathed her with dubious looks.

She hurriedly dropped back into her seat, then hunched over and whispered above the radio, "Is that you, Corporal?" But she couldn't hear a response, and when she turned up the volume, the static only got worse, causing the father across the aisle to glare at her in annoyance. The girl frowned and stirred a little in her sleep.

Holding the radio, she stood up again. The passengers had all gone back to their own seats and their own pastimes and didn't seem to think there was anything particularly suspicious about her. Even so, she worried about the gazes of the people around her as she went quickly down the aisle toward the door to the car behind them.

The moment she opened the door and stepped out onto the pitch-dark deck, the noise from the wheels banged against her eardrums and a cutting, cold wind disturbed her hair. She hurried to close the door, then plastered herself to the train's wall to get out of the wind, and shouted loud enough to be heard over the surrounding noise.

"Corporal. Corporal, is that you!? Can you hear me?"

She turned the radio up to its highest volume and waited a bit; a broken reply came through the static.

"... *Kieli ... can you hear me ...?*"

It had only been a few days, but she had missed the staticky voice terribly. Kieli held back the tears that were about to spill from her eyes, brought her face close to the radio, and began to speak. "Corporal, how? Did you come back?"

"... *Kieli ... can you hear me ...? Go to the freight car ...*"

"Corporal?"

But the radio didn't answer and only repeated the same line: "... *Kieli ... can you hear me ...? Go to the freight car ...*" It wasn't much of a conversation. "The freight car ...?" Kieli leaned out from the deck and stared at the cars lined up behind it. She squinted into the darkness, relying on the square yellow lights that fringed the windows of the passenger cars. There were three passenger cars behind her current location, and after that, two cargo cars were stuck to the end.

"*. . . Kieli . . . go to the freight car . . .*" the radio's voice continued, like a chant.

Gazing at the freight car she saw behind her, Kieli nodded silently. She lowered the volume on the radio, hung it from her neck, and crossed the deck to the next car.

She had not a single reason to hesitate.

When she came out onto the deck of the last passenger car, closed the door, and finally saw the freight car that came next in the dull light filtering through the small window behind her, she nevertheless felt a bit of hesitation.

The deck of the freight car in front of her was no more than a simple foothold, and most importantly, there wasn't a door in front of her like there had been on the passenger cars. There was a big sliding door in about the middle of the sidewall for loading cargo, and it seemed that was the only entrance. Also, there was a wide space between the two cars, and it looked as if she would need to jump to get to the next one.

"*. . . Kieli . . . go to the freight car . . .*"

"I know, Corporal. It's okay. I can get there." The voice from the radio was still only one-way, but she said it clearly out loud in order to convince herself.

She took a deep breath and swallowed, then summoned her determination and leapt from the deck.

As the tips of her toes reached the measly little deck, she clung to the handrail with both hands, and moved to the side wall without hesitation. Her hair and clothes fluttered madly in the wind as she gradually made her way along the side wall, using the sliding door's rail as a foothold. It was actually fortunate that she couldn't see her feet in the darkness. If she caught sight of the train track racing under them at such a high speed, she would undoubtedly have frozen and not been able to move.

"Just a little further . . ."

She reached out and somehow managed to grab the lock lever on the sliding door. When she opened it, wind filled her skirt and it puffed up around her.

The bottom of her shoes left her foothold.

"Ah!" The wind immediately carried her short involuntary scream away, and her body was blown backward as if following it.

Just in the nick of time, a hand suddenly reached through the opening in the door and grabbed her wrist. Except for her one arm, her body floated in the air for one second, then she was yanked forward and tumbled into the freight car, falling facedown onto the chest of the hand's owner.

She knew instantly whose hand it was, of course. Slender but rough, powerful, big hands.

"Harvey, Harvey!" she repeated the name ecstatically as she hurried to get up; "Har — !" Then, when she raised her face and saw him, Kieli's expression froze.

There in front of her was indeed the copper-haired young man she had longed to see. But there was no emotion on his face, and his eyes of the same color were empty, looking nowhere.

". . . Harvey?"

Kieli watched in blank amazement as the dark green ghost of a soldier slowly emerged from his body and disappeared into the radio, as if it was sucking him in. That instant, Harvey's neck, which had somehow kept itself straight until then, dropped to an unnatural angle; he lost his strength and fell over.

Kieli wound up catching his massive weight, and, unable to support it completely, she was pushed down and fell onto her posterior. The copper head that leaned against her slid from Kieli's shoulder to the floor with a dull thud.

". . . Eh . . . ?" As she sat there motionless, she looked down at Harvey's body collapsed on the floor, and Kieli's breath stopped. She timidly reached out and tried touching his cheek. She automatically pulled her hand back at its chilling cold and its strange texture, and her fingers left a dent where they'd touched him.

He felt exactly like a corpse.

". . . N . . . o."

"Calm down, Kieli. Don't be alarmed. Listen carefully." Kieli was about to panic; it was the voice from the radio hanging around her neck that kept her tied to reality. Before she realized, it had stopped its one-way chant and now actually addressed her.

"Corporal, Corporal," she brought her face to the radio, clinging to it with both hands. "Harvey's, why, how . . ."

"I possessed him and moved him here. Damn, do you know how hard it was? You can't walk with a body like that. It's great that I snuck onto the train, but it's gonna be impossible to walk around anymore. That's why I rode the guerrilla station's frequency and sent my voice to you."

"I don't understand. I don't understand what you're saying!" Kieli raised her voice, more and more confused at his sudden explanation. The force of her shout brought her tears overflowing with it, and all the feelings she had been forcing back flooded out in a jumble.

"Never mind that, Harvey's not moving. How did he get like this? I want to talk to Harvey. I wanted to see him one more time . . ."

"I told you *to calm down! Crying's not gonna help anything!"* The radio raised his voice to match hers, spitting his staticky features at Kieli from the speaker at point-blank range and

causing her to pull back. Still sobbing uncontrollably, she earnestly wiped her tears and listened carefully, trying to understand what he was telling her.

"In his current condition, Herbie is just a corpse. We're gonna get his heart's core back. Most likely, he has it. The one commanding the Church Soldiers."

"He . . . ? Who . . . ?"

"The guy you boarded the train with. I saw you both from the platform's shadow. So my hunch was right. Damn, we should have been more cautious about him."

"Joachim . . . ?" she almost continued but stopped herself.

"I haven't told you this before, Kieli, but it's something I heard from Herbie once. The Church isn't after the Undying because they're criminals of war or because their existence goes against God or anything like that. That's just what they tell the believers. The Undyings' cores are the last fruits of the energy civilization from before the War, and those guys just want the technology and resources from them."

"That's why they . . . ?"

His story shocked her, but while she listened, she regained some of her composure and looked down again at Harvey's body lying next to her. His right leg and shoulder were completely gone, and as if that wasn't horrible enough, his shirt was open to reveal a hole gouged carelessly in his chest, coal-tar-like blood staining his clothes.

She saw in him the image of the Undying that was killed in front of her seven years ago, when her grandmother was still alive.

". . . How can they? So cruel . . ."

The tears she had once stifled threatened to overflow again, and she bit her lip. She reached out both hands and embraced his head, his hair reeking of coal-tar blood. When she asked him before, he said with a calm expression that he could ignore the pain. But that didn't mean it didn't hurt, being torn up like this.

"Kieli, you can cry later. Can you do it? Or you can pretend you don't know anything, and just go back to the passenger car. You have that choice. If you do, I won't say anything."

"Are you saying that because you think I'd do that?" she asked through her tears. The radio readily replied, *"I called you because I don't."* Kieli smiled just a little and carefully placed Harvey's head on the floor. She didn't think that he would feel any cold, but she took off her coat and laid it over him anyway. She gently closed both of his empty eyes with the palm of her hand, leaned close, and quietly whispered, "Wait for me."

She took on a stiff expression, made sure the radio hung from her neck, and stood up.

"Guards," Kieli whispered, peeking into the passenger car from the small window in the door, and ducked back down onto the deck. Two Church Soldiers stood in front of the door leading from the first passenger car to the Church's car. Kieli was clinging to the deck on the opposite end. The passengers all sat normally, riding the train, but apparently no one had the courage to sit directly in front of Church Soldiers, and they all seemed to bundle in the back.

"Well, that figures," the radio answered beneath her chin, then, as if tired of thinking about it, *"Well, how are we gonna do this?"*

"We'll get there from above," Kieli said, without waiting for him to continue, and looked up at the roof of the passenger car. A simple work ladder was installed in the wall, and it seemed as though she could climb up from there. She placed her foot on it without hesitating.

"*Hey, are you serious? This is dangerous.*"

"But there's no other way," she answered lightly, climbing the ladder. When she stuck her face out on the roof, a sudden gust hit her. "Wait a second . . ." She ducked down for a minute to get out of the wind and retied the cord on the radio so it would be too short for the wind to throw it around.

Then she braced herself, scrambled up onto the roof, and started to crawl along it on her belly. The fierce, skin-piercing headwind blasted mercilessly at her hair and skirt; and her hands and feet, which had frozen instantly, almost slipped countless times. She resolved that when this was over, she would stop wearing skirts, and she would cut her hair short to keep it out of the way.

"*You okay, Kieli?*" came the radio's muffled voice from under her stomach.

"Yeah. Just a little further . . ." The wind sent her answer flying behind them.

As she frantically moved onward, her fingers caught the edge of the roof on the other side. She used all the strength in her arms to pull her body forward and practically slid down the simple ladder to the front deck below.

That instant, the back of the Church Soldier's head that she saw through the small window into the passenger car abruptly turned around; she screamed inwardly and plastered herself to the wall. She waited a while, pushing back her heart as it tried to jump out of her and holding her breath. After a little bit, she looked and saw that the soldier in the window had his back to her again.

"Whew. All's clear. Let's go."

"*You're pretty incredible, you know that . . . ?*" the radio said, impressed.

"How do you mean?" Kieli answered briefly, already starting her next move. She thought she sounded kind of like Harvey, if she did say so herself. Harvey's frank tone, his voice with its controlled pitch — a low voice that purred a little in his throat and sounded a little staticky. She wanted to hear that voice one more time. She got the feeling that desire was connected to the risks she was currently taking that surprised even her.

The darkness of night enveloped her surroundings, and only the rushing wind, the roar of the wheels, and the sharp vibrations under her feet conveyed to her that the scenery on either side of her was passing by very quickly.

There was a black iron door in front of her. The roof was higher than on the passenger cars, and it stood as if to block her way.

She checked the window behind her, ducked down, jumped across the deck, and clung to the door on the other side. This door had a window, too, but at Kieli's height, she couldn't see inside it. She could only just barely tell that there was no one to be seen on the other side. She grabbed the lever and tried pulling it; the door was heavy, but she managed to move it, and when she had it open just far enough to fit herself through, she slipped inside.

The door gave in to its weight and closed on its own, and the roar from outside instantly went quiet.

There was one more deck on the inside. A single light bulb hung from the ceiling; it illuminated the narrow space, swinging with the vibrations of the train. There was a small door to her left, but it looked like it led to a bathroom. The door to the next car was farther ahead, slightly to the right. This time, she could see through the small window by standing tiptoe.

A narrow aisle went up to the door on the other side. Dull electric lights lit the aisle at equal intervals, and doors lined the left wall at those same intervals. It looked like they were private rooms.

She quietly opened and closed the door into the car and stepped into the aisle.

That instant, she heard voices from the room closest to her and instinctively made as if to escape, but once she turned on her heels, she realized that they were just having a friendly chat that had nothing to do with her. She peered through the room's window and saw three or four soldiers wearing only half their armor, sitting and talking. She stole past, suppressing her leaping heartbeat.

The next room appeared to be for storage; boxes of all sizes lay in disordered stacks in the gloom.

She was about to pass that room, too, when, without warning, she heard the sound of the door opening behind her. She just barely caught her scream and swallowed it as it reached her throat, and at once jumped into the storage room. Clutching the radio, she fastened herself to the inside wall. Armored footsteps with spurs approached. . . .

Humans must be a pretty hopeless bunch if there are guys that would pay enough for this rock for me to buy a sandship with it. And after you destroyed most of them in a war you started yourselves. You used to be rolling in them.

Lying on the simple bed in his dimly lit room, Joachim gazed at the black stone he carried in one hand, a bored expression on his face. It was a rough, black rock, about the size of a grown man's fist, but looking at it closely, it was easy to tell that this was no ordinary stone. Sockets for connections to all sorts of organic cables, from thick veins to capillaries, lined one side, and the amber light imprisoned inside blinked on and off like a heartbeat.

Inside the amber was the true form of the Undying's power source, and organic cables connected it to their blood vessels and organic tissue, furnishing them with semipermanent energy and extraordinary healing abilities.

The few records from before the War contained the somewhat plausible explanation that there were special minute particles containing cell-repairing functions included in the blood the core sent through the body, and whenever they activated, they turned into a black tarlike substance — but the technology to manufacture them, the research facilities, and even the materials used to make them were all lost in that long, ridiculous War, so it wasn't like there was any way to reproduce them, whether they knew how they worked or not.

"You're pathetic, Ephraim," he murmured with a smirk, throwing the core unceremoniously into the air and catching it again. He derived pleasure from the thought that the higher-ups would probably scream if they saw him treating it the way he was.

"Well, think of it as providing for my peaceful life and be happy. I guess I could goof off for thirty years. Maybe I'll go ahead and shoot for building a spaceship? We do have the time to travel infinite space for eternity, after all."

The thought he so casually put into words strangely caught his fancy, and he grinned to himself for a while, but he erased the smile without warning. He narrowed his eyes and glared at the stone in his hand.

"Hey, what's the deal, Ephraim? Your toy really pisses me off. I'm sitting right in front of her, and she looks right through me. That little girl doesn't think about anything but you."

A girl who shows no signs of rejection toward Undying — he had thought she'd help him relieve some boredom, but it was taking more time to win her over than he expected. *She was so attached to Ephraim, so what's her problem with me? That's no fun. She pisses me off. Ephraim, that little girl, the higher-ups — every single one of them does nothing but piss me off.*

The annoyance in his stomach reached an abrupt climax, and he bolted upright, raised the core above his head, and flung it against the wall (if the higher-ups saw it, they would undoubtedly faint). The core hit the shutters drawn over the car window, denting them some, and fell onto the flooring.

The black stone shook slightly, rattling with the floor's vibrations. He glared down at it and spat, "Serves you right." Then, as he swore to himself at the feeling that this had been an extremely empty victory, spurred footsteps approached from outside in the aisle. The footsteps stopped in front of his room, and he heard a knock, along with a soldier's muffled voice.

"Joachim."

"Ugh, annoying . . ." he spat, sending a sideways scowl at the door as he picked up the core, stuffed it halfheartedly into the coat he had taken off, and got up from his seat.

"Keep up the good work. What's the matter?" By the time he opened the door in response, he had stuck on his "kind and trustworthy young Church leader candidate" face.

The soldier standing in the door hesitated inside his mask, then said, "The young lady you brought with you has disappeared from the passenger car. . . ."

"Disappeared?"

"Yes. She's not there," he said as if he was just asking someone to hit him. Joachim managed to keep himself from obliging, pushed the soldier out of the way, and flew out of the room. *That little girl!*

". . . *Whew. That took years off my life,*" the radio in her arms grumbled once the sounds of hurried footsteps running by, then the door to the next car opening and closing, had died down. "You're already dead," Kieli replied simply, then stood up, looked through the small window to make sure no one was there, and set out into the aisle again.

From the distance of the voices, she figured that the room the Church Soldier had visited and Joachim had just left was the one farthest down. She ignored the doors in between and ran at once to that room, going at a trot so that her feet wouldn't make any noise.

Peering through the small window, she saw that it looked like the other rooms, but somewhat fancier, with a desk, a chair, and a simple bed. She checked the doors to the other cars on her right and left again, then slipped inside and closed the door behind her.

She instinctively held her breath as she scanned the inside of the dimly lit room. There was a big Boston bag and a trunk crammed under the bed, but there wasn't anything else worth mentioning that might be called luggage. She glanced back through the window behind her, stepped farther inside the room, knelt on the floor, and pulled the bags out from under the bed.

She rummaged through the Boston bag first, but all that was inside were clothes, books, and daily necessities. Next she was about to open the trunk, but stopped.

"It's locked," she muttered, not sure what to do.

"Kieli, lift me up a little."

After thinking about the significance of the unfriendly instructions, she took the radio in both hands and raised it up a bit. The speaker released a more reserved shock wave than usual, but it still made a fairly loud *kaboom*, denting the front of the trunk.

"Pretty handy, eh? I might have what it takes to be a thief."

"All you did was break it . . ."

Half-exasperated at the boast, Kieli stuck her hands and the toes of her shoes in the gap made when the trunk twisted, and used all her strength to pry it open. She had no right to tell off the radio; she was using a pretty violent method herself.

"*Is that it?*" the radio asked in a somewhat eager voice, the minute they peered into the trunk.

There was a sturdy-looking metal case inside. Her heart pounded with anticipation as Kieli picked it up in both hands, but her hopes immediately came crashing down. The case was unlocked, and it was empty. And yet there was space for a round object about ten centimeters in diameter inside, and it was clearly for keeping the core inside.

"*If you think about it, it's not necessarily in his luggage. He might always keep it on him.*"

"Then how do I get it back?"

There was a pause after her question. "*So it's hopeless . . .*" came the radio's dejected voice. Kieli sighed, too, and sat down on the bed. This was no time to be taking a break, but she had no idea what she should do next. She was so ready to help Harvey, but in the end, there was nothing she could do. She bit her lip, resenting her powerlessness.

As she clenched her fist, it grabbed something.

"Wha . . . ?"

She dropped her gaze down beside her and saw the coat Joachim had been wearing, left in an unceremonious heap on his bed. Something tugged at her consciousness, and she instinctively picked it up.

A black thing rolled out onto the bed.

". . . There it is," she muttered in shock after a minute of speechlessness. Just like the Undying's heart she had seen when she was small, it was a black stone containing a dull amber-colored light.

"*What's it doing there . . . ?*" The radio, too, sounded deflated.

Kieli reached out with shaking hands and picked it up. It was profoundly heavy in her hands, and conveyed a warmth in time with the blinking of the amber light. In its warmth and touch, she could definitely feel the owner of the hand that held hers on the way back from the carnival. "Treat it with more respect . . ." she murmured hoarsely, holding it to her heart.

"Hurry. Let's go back."

"Yeah."

She nodded at the radio's voice and hurried to stand up.

Suddenly the private room's door opened violently. She froze, half-sitting, and turned her head to see Joachim standing there with several armored Church Soldiers behind him.

"My, my. We have quite the little thief here, I see."

Joachim cast his eyes on what was in Kieli's hands and grinned. Still smiling, one of his cheeks twitched. Kieli fixed a glare on the man and forced the core into her skirt pocket. *Bear with it a little, Harvey,* she apologized inwardly.

"Give it back."

"Why should I give it to you? This is Harvey's."

"You're a good girl, so give it back before you get hurt. Do you know just how valuable that stone is?"

Joachim held out his hand and took a step forward. Kieli took a step back. That went on for only a few steps before her back hit the wall. *"Kieli. Lure him closer,"* the radio whispered in a voice only Kieli could hear, then added one more thing. *"Hold your ground."*

Kieli turned her eyes upward to gaze at Joachim and waited firmly against the wall. The young priest plastered a smile, but a strangely twisted one, on his face and approached slowly.

"There's a good girl."

His extended fingers touched Kieli's cheek — and in an instant, the radio's speaker roared, releasing an earsplitting ball of high-pitched sound.

A shock wave of maximum output hit Joachim directly in the face and blew him to the wall in the aisle outside, taking the soldiers behind with him. The recoil blasted Kieli backward; her back hit the wall, knocking the wind out of her, and she coughed violently.

"Run!"

At the same time the radio gave its instructions, she kicked the wall and flew from the room, still coughing. Not even glancing at the pile of people lying against the wall, she turned right and ran to the door that led to the car behind them.

By the time she heard an angry voice behind her yelling, "After her!" she had already passed over the deck.

One side of his head heard a soldier's voice yell, "After her!" and hurried footsteps. He sensed someone crouching diagonally above him. Then he heard a gasp of, "It's no good. He's dead!"

Joachim suddenly opened his eye.

"Eep!" the soldier that had been peering into his face yelped, falling back onto his rear end. Joachim lifted the top half of his body as if nothing was wrong. The two soldiers he had taken into the wall with him were unconscious and not moving. They might have died with the impact, but he didn't care.

He touched his face with one hand and heard an unpleasant squishing sound; pieces of flesh stuck to his hand. "Kieli. Now you've done it . . ."

When he spoke, air whistled through his cheek where the flesh had fallen off.

He staggered to his feet. The soldier beside him must have been paralyzed with fear; he remained on the ground, looking up at him, his teeth chattering. Joachim glanced expressionlessly at the shameful sight and snatched the carbonization gun from the soldier's hands.

Metallic footsteps chased after her. Kieli ran down the aisles of the passenger cars, occasionally turning back to look behind her.

The passengers, curious, started up to see what all the commotion was about, but when they saw the gun-wielding soldiers following Kieli, they gave short screams and ducked back into the shadows of their seats. She wanted to have the radio shoot out another shock wave to buy them some distance, but she couldn't afford to hurt the innocent passengers, so at any rate, she had no choice but to get out of the passenger cars as fast as she could.

This time, when she got out onto the deck of the last passenger car, she didn't have time to think about being scared and jumped to the freight car, using the sliding door's rail as footing to edge along the side wall as she did the first time she'd come.

Church Soldiers appeared on the passenger car's deck. When she caught sight of them out of the corner of her eye, Kieli was already sliding into the freight car through the opening in the door.

She closed the sliding door, using a nearby piece of iron to block the door in what little way she could. She didn't take the time to catch her breath as she turned and ran to Harvey, hidden in the shadows of the cargo. Kneeling beside him, she tore her coat off of him, and, not surprisingly, Harvey lay there exactly as before, showing no signs of even turning in his sleep.

She pulled the core impatiently from her skirt, held it in both hands, and gazed at it for a while.

"Corporal, will this really help him? Will Harvey come back?"

"We won't know unless we try. If it doesn't work, we'll deal with it then."

Kieli gulped and nodded silently. She slowly moved the core near the hole in Harvey's chest. She thought, if it didn't work, then this time, she wouldn't mind dying with him. But she knew Harvey would get mad if he found out she'd said it.

Even so, she couldn't help her hands' shaking, and they became more unsteady as she timidly pushed the core where it was supposed to go.

She got the feeling that the amber light within the stone blinked a little bit brighter than usual. She involuntarily held the breath she had inhaled and watched over him, as if in prayer.

But that was it.

"It didn't work . . . ?" came the radio's discouraged voice.

"We don't know yet. I'm sure . . ." Kieli murmured, trying to reassure herself, but she couldn't even convince herself, and her voice trailed off. She hung her head and bit her lip.

A sense of despair spread throughout her heart. It really was useless to pray to God. If only the devil would show up, she would gladly make a pact with him.

Just then, an angry muffled voice yelling, "Open up!" and the sound of violent pounding on the door echoed from the other side of the wall. She heard a gunshot; smoke rose from one spot, and the door caved in. Three soldiers trampled down the twisted iron and came into the car, one after another.

Still on one knee, Kieli turned her body around and shielded Harvey. The radio's speaker roared. A shock wave hit the last soldier to try to get through the door, and he let out a low scream as he lost his balance and went flying into the darkness outside. No time passed before the second shock wave swelled around the radio.

But instead of a second shock wave, the speaker only let out a forlorn puff of air before spouting black smoke. *"Sorry, Kieli. I forced too much power earl . . ."* The radio's voice cut off abruptly with a short tearing of static.

"Corporal . . ." Kieli dropped her gaze to the radio for an instant, but, sensing someone, she immediately raised her face again.

When the remaining two soldiers entered her vision, approaching with their guns trained on her, she kicked the floor and tackled one of them in the abdomen, with no fear for the consequences. She wasn't able to knock him down, but she kept going and got his chest, grabbing his carbonization gun by the barrel and hugging it to her.

"Why you, little girl!"

An armored glove grabbed her and hung her up by her arm; her feet floated in the air. "Let go!" she screamed, and kicked the soldier in the shin as hard as she could, but his hard armor didn't budge. She only succeeded in numbing her own leg.

"Hey, take a look at this." The other soldier had approached the cargo and now turned his voice, muffled through his mask, to his partner. "Isn't that the Undying we killed at the abandoned mine? How did she bring his corpse in here?" he said in surprise as he looked down at the body lying in the shadows of the cargo and casually poked the copper-colored head with his toe.

"Stop it!" Kieli shouted, flailing her legs all the more furiously. "Don't touch him! Don't touch Harvey!"

"Stop struggling!" an irritated voice spat at her from above, and she felt a dull shock on the side of her head. Her vision went dark for a second, and by the time she realized that something had hit her, she had been flung violently to the floor.

Trying to keep her head from reeling, she sent a look of uncontrolled hostility at the soldiers.

"Uwaaahh!" the soldier by the cargo suddenly cried out in shock.

Kieli turned her head in surprise to see the corpse suddenly move and tackle the soldier with his shoulder. Knocked backward, the soldier slid along the floor to the open doorway and flew outside, taking the twisted iron door with him. His muffled scream shrank in an instant and disappeared beyond the darkness.

"Y-you bastard!" Taken aback, the other soldier panicked and turned his gun on Harvey, but by then Harvey was already making his next move. He snatched up the gun the other soldier had thrown down in his left hand, used the floor as support and, still lying on the ground, pulled the trigger.

A dull gunshot rang out, reverberating against the walls and ceiling. The shot hit the soldier in the chest, knocking him back to the opposite wall; he collapsed against it and stopped moving.

The series of actions took place in the blink of an eye, while Kieli sat on the floor gaping, her hands on her temples. She noticed that Harvey had stopped moving where he was, exhausted; she gasped and pulled herself together.

"Harvey!"

Harvey had thrown the carbonization gun away from him and was merely lying listlessly on the floor, as if he really had been dead there the whole time. He made no sign of even twitching in response to her voice. "Harvey, wake up . . ." Almost in tears from the anxiety that came welling up inside her again, she crawled toward him on her hands.

"Wake up. Come on, please . . ." When she knelt beside him and brought her pleading face to his, "Wah!"

The left arm that had been flung to the floor abruptly moved and yanked Kieli's neck closer. It took Kieli by surprise, and she collapsed into his chest.

Before her eyes, the core blinked its amber light, and had started a weak, but definite, pulse. The coal-tar blood wrapped around the torn organic cables at a sluggish speed, putting them back together.

"Where ... are we ...?" she heard a voice above her head that spoke haltingly, as if still somewhat lacking in strength. Kieli's head was fixed in place, but she lifted it a little to look up at Harvey's chin.

"The Church Soldiers' train. The Corporal brought you here. Then we got your core back together, and ..." She became more and more inarticulate as she started to explain, then Harvey's hand, still wrapped around her neck, touched her temple; she stopped talking and blinked. The spot where the soldier hit her was a little warm, but it hurt so little that even she had forgotten it for a minute.

"Oh, I'm fine. It's just a bump ..."

"Shut up. What are you doing?" Harvey curtly rejected her attempt to dismiss her pain. "Look, you. Why do always end up sticking your nose into everything? This girl has no idea how I felt when I sent her back ..." The last part trailed off, as if he was talking to himself, and she didn't hear most of it. She only felt the strength of his arm that held her so tightly she almost couldn't breathe and the faint warmth of his body; Kieli pressed her face into the chest of his tobacco-scented shirt and closed her eyes for a bit.

"Kieli ..."

Joachim walked slowly down the aisles of the passenger cars, the carbonization gun dangling from one hand. Sometimes he tottered on his feet. With half of his vision and hearing blown away, his senses were unclear, as if there was a membrane over them. It was possible that half of his brain had been blown away as well.

To the right and left of his blurred vision, humans watched him in fear; their stares got on his nerves. There were even brats who started crying — how irritating. He would kill them all later.

But right now, this group of insects didn't matter — his only prey was the little girl on the other side.

"Kieli . . ." Joachim muttered her name like a curse and kept walking.

"Grab on." Kieli jumped onto the deck from the freight car's side wall, then hurriedly offered a hand to Harvey, coming behind her. She dragged his large body onto the deck using both arms, then breathed a sigh of relief. At any rate, Harvey was still in no condition to stand, and even in the short time they spent walking along the side wall, he almost fell from the foothold dozens of times.

They had left the first freight car and moved onto the deck of the freight car behind it. The plan was to detach the last freight car. Harvey by himself would be one thing, but it would be reckless for him to jump off holding Kieli at this speed. Kieli would be too much baggage for Harvey in his current state.

"Kieli, hold me up a little more. Sorry for the trouble."

As soon as he crawled up onto the deck, Harvey leaned over the edge of the car and started looking for the coupler's release lever. Kieli didn't need him to tell her — she clung to Harvey's back to make sure he didn't slip and fall off. The radio stuck between them was still broken, and Kieli felt something missing in the lack of the Corporal's complaints.

"If we walk as far as the transfer station and slip into the crowd, we can escape," Harvey spoke quickly as he reached for the release lever on the other side of the coupler. Kieli got the feeling he had asked her something after that, but the sounds of the wheels and wind drowned out his voice. "What?" Kieli asked, leaning close.

He turned his head halfway around, "Do you want to go east or west?"

"Eh?" Kieli gazed back at him blankly. ". . . The Sand Ocean. I want to see what it's like to ride a boat," she answered after a small pause. Harvey smiled and said in his usual light tone, "All right. I'll get you on a boat."

After taking a few seconds to process the meaning of that statement, Kieli brightened and asked over his shoulder, "Really? You'll take me with you?"

"What are you talking about? There's nothing we can do about it now. I at least have to take responsibility for making you a wanted criminal," Harvey started to say as he resumed the act of pulling the lever but cut himself off in the middle. ". . . That's not what I mean. Correction." He stopped his hands, turned around one more time, made a face as if he was thinking of what to say for a second, then said again, "Will you come with me, Kieli?"

Kieli didn't hesitate to give a big nod, and buried her cheek in his back in front of her.

"Kieli . . . !" That was when a voice calling her name, like a curse, came flying with the wind from ahead.

The sense of urgency that had begun to leave the two of them came rushing back. Still grabbing the back of Harvey's coat, Kieli twisted her body and peered toward the front of the train from the shadows of the side wall. A man with the appearance of a priest was coming toward them along the side of the car ahead of them, the sleeves of his long robe fluttering in the wind.

Her eyes barely met his blue-gray one. "Kieli, I won't let you get away . . ." The man smiled, his eyes glaring. Only, there was only one eye — in fact, half his head was split, and she could see something reddish-black and pulpy through his sunken skull.

"Harvey . . . !" His ghastly appearance gave Kieli chills, and she drew her head back. When she did, she heard a short metallic sound by Harvey's hands, and the tightly clenched fists of the couplers came free.

"It's okay. Hurry over there."

At Harvey's urging, Kieli jumped over to the rear freight car and — "Hurry" — immediately turned around to lend him a hand, but she grabbed only empty air. Harvey stayed crouched on the deck, making no attempt to jump over.

There was the clunk of a heavy shock, and the cars started to separate.

"Harvey! No. Why!?"

"Go on ahead for a sec. I have some minor business with that idiot."

"No! You're lying! I'm staying with you!" Kieli wailed and tried to go back, but his sharp cry of, "Stay there!" and his strong arms held her back. Harvey brought his face close to hers and whispered in a quiet, low voice, "We'll get on a boat, Kieli. I promise."

She felt as if the howl of the wind, the thunder of the wheels, and all the sounds blowing violently around them stopped for a brief moment. His copper eyes almost touched her, and she felt his long sigh on her lips.

The next instant, he pushed her shoulders, and she flew back onto the rear car. The scene before her, Harvey's face as he watched her go, rapidly grew farther away. The wind came flying back again, drowning out her cry so that it didn't even reach her own ears.

"Damn it! Kieli!" Joachim had made it from the side wall to the deck. He spat and fired a shot at the train tracks to vent his frustration. The separated car was already far away, disappearing on the other side of the darkness.

"Stop the train! Now!"

There were no longer any soldiers following him — a fact which made him even angrier — and when he turned on his heels, bellowing, an arm suddenly appeared from behind him and wrapped itself around his neck — from the shadow of the opposite wall! Damn it, every single one of them!

He twisted his face in rage and looked behind him. Nothing came into the half of his vision that remained, so he turned his neck even farther and heard the sound of a sinew snapping. Then finally he could see the person behind him.

"Yo, Joachim. I hear you took real good care of Kieli."

"Ephraim! Why you . . . how . . . !?"

Over his shoulder, he saw those loathsome copper-colored eyes. He thought he'd killed him, but the bastard went and came back to life, as if he didn't know when to quit. Joachim didn't even bother to hide his annoyance.

"What were you planning to do with her?"

"Heh. You sure are attached to her. That little girl's just gonna die soon, anyway," he retorted, spitting; the other man narrowed his eyes in displeasure. It was a strangely pleasant feeling to make someone he despised feel miserable, and Joachim cackled.

"I feel so sorry for you when you're disappointed, so I took her for you. You should be grateful. But I don't need her

anymore. She's not as much fun as I thought she'd be. What will I do? Should I catch her and kill her? Or sell her to slave traders . . . ?" He only intended to string together whatever offensive things came to mind, but as he talked, he started to mean it more and more. He was about to say as many more things as he could come up with when a voice interrupted.

"That's enough. Stop talking."

The other man suddenly did something he never would have expected. He reached over Joachim's shoulder, grabbed his gun, turned it 180 degrees, and pulled the trigger — it was like he was ignoring the possibility that the shot would go right through and hit him, too.

"You bastard . . !"

The shock blasted through the center of Joachim's body, and he flew backward. He took the enemy behind with him, and they were both thrown off the deck, tangled together, into the rushing darkness.

"Guh . . ."

In the pitch darkness, the cold sensation of the ground under Harvey's cheek confirmed to him that, somehow, he was still living on this earth.

After being tossed out like a scrap of paper blown around in the wind and then rammed into the ground, he somersaulted quite a distance until his whole body crashed thoroughly into the face of a rock. He had exhausted the willpower to block the pain, but, perhaps fortunately, he didn't have many nerves left with which to feel it; his whole body was heavy as if paralyzed, and all he felt was a throbbing in the core of his brain.

He gritted his teeth and pulled himself up. He tried to support himself with his right arm, but couldn't find it and collapsed to the earth, shoulder-first. He had taken the shot that pierced Joachim, and his right arm had been cut off partway through the upper arm and had gone off somewhere. And he thought he had just barely dodged it.

Harvey managed to pick himself up with his left arm and looked out over the darkness around him. He could vaguely make out the shadow of someone lying a few meters ahead, and he dragged his body close to it. The priestly man lay there, his head and limbs bent in what were originally impossible directions. Smoke rose from the middle of his chest, and the smell of burning wafted around him.

He took another step, and the tip of his shoe kicked something.

When he dropped his gaze and strained his eyes, he saw a black stone on the ground, the size of a fist. Half of its surface smoldered after turning to carbon, and inside, an amber light blinked feebly. He stooped and reached out his hand to pick it up —

That instant, Joachim's arm flashed in the corner of his vision, and the hand that reached from it grabbed his wrist with an abnormally strong grip.

"— !"

He started and froze in place, but the next instant, there was a small fizzle, and the light inside the core disappeared before his eyes.

Just past his outstretched fingertips, the stone was reduced to cinders and crumbled.

He raised his eyes and saw that Joachim had stopped moving, his one remaining blue-gray eye wide open, glaring at him.

"Moron . . ." he murmured, and peeled Joachim's fingers off his wrist. His finger marks left a distinct bruise, and for no good reason he was firmly convinced it wouldn't disappear for a while.

After that, he tried with a grunt to raise his upper body, but his energy drained away instantaneously, and he crumpled on the spot.

Once he had lowered his hips, there was no getting them back up. There was a heavy, hot mass of something in the center of his head, and he felt that if he closed his eyes, this time he really would be able to sleep, and, lured by the whisper of, "You can sleep now," he started to close his eyelids.

Suddenly, he remembered something important.

"Oh yeah, I made a promise . . ."

He staggered to his feet. He couldn't see the train track. And he'd lost sight of which direction to go. He didn't even know if he could make it there. Even so, he started to walk in the direction where he thought he might see a light somewhere. It was no more than a hunch, but he could clearly see in his brain the sand-colored light of the sky that shone through the ceiling of the abandoned mine, and he got the feeling that if he went to it, she would take his hand and pull him out of the long, long flow of time that he had drifted through alone.

GOD, IF YOU'RE HERE

The train bound for the Sand Ocean arrived from the west, and the transfer station suddenly filled with noise.

Travelers passed busily through, carrying big bags, a bit of fatigue, and more than anything, high hopes for their journeys. No one paid any attention to the lone girl leaning against a wall in the waiting area near the ticket barrier, watching the train.

To be more precise, she wasn't alone; she had someone to talk to hanging from her neck.

"Maybe it's about time we better be giving up, too. Those guys've already stopped searching."

"Yeah . . ." Kieli answered absently, casually casting her gaze at the flow of people coming and going on the platform.

It had been about two weeks. The Church Soldiers held an investigation for the first few days, but they had abandoned that, too, and the station regained the bright everyday conversations of its citizens.

From the beginning, no one suspected Kieli very much. She had already stopped wearing the boarding school uniform she had grown so accustomed to. She wore very unfeminine clothing — a light down jacket and jeans — and she had shortened her long hair. She had cut it herself using a knife, so it wasn't very attractive, but it made her feel much better.

Upbeat music flowed from the radio's speaker at a faint volume that only Kieli could hear. The radio had been broken countless times, so the sound quality really was terrible, but to Kieli, the static was actually rather pleasant. And she liked the Corporal's voice, too, as it rode the melody and spoke to her.

"Are you sure it's okay, Corporal? I could take you back to the abandoned mine again, you know."

"You guys are nothing but trouble; I couldn't disappear in peace. I've just about given up and started thinking of this radio as my original body."

"I'll be careful with you so you don't break anymore."

The radio's grumpy, but slightly bashful, voice was so funny Kieli couldn't suppress a small laugh, but the people around her increased as departing passengers blended with arriving ones, so she shut her mouth.

She nodded when the radio suggested giving up, but once the day was over, she would most likely come back tomorrow and see the trains off as they headed the east. And when tomorrow was over, the day after, too. No, she was thinking she would take the radio and head out the day after tomorrow. There was no use waiting around here, doing nothing, forever.

She wanted to be someone who could travel on her own. So that someday, when she met him again, she would be a little stronger.

"Let's go home."

"Had enough today?"

"Yeah. I'll come again tomorrow, and after that I'll give up."

Kieli didn't wait for the train to go. She left the wall and started to walk with the current of arriving passengers heading for the station's exit. There was a wide stairway at the front of the passage, and a girl wearing a hat ran up the stairs, jumping up and down in excitement. Her mother came after her, carrying their bags.

"What do you think was wrong with that man, Mama?"

"He's dead. Someone will call for help; it's okay."

Kieli happened to pass by the conversation, then stopped and turned around. The girl skipped around her mother and said cheerfully, "Eehh? He's not dead. He's alive."

". . . . . . !" The second Kieli heard that, she started running to the exit. She dashed through the hall, pushing aside people who scowled at her in annoyance. When she got to the top of the staircase, she could see a square cutout of outside light under her eyes. Passersby buried the stairway, but at the very bottom, for some reason, there was an empty space in just one corner by the wall; people avoided it as they walked by.

She impatiently ran down the steps two at a time. The radio bounced against her belly.

Please, God. She prayed inside her heart. *You don't have to be the Church's God. But if there is a God on this planet, please take off that completely flawless, impartial mask, just for now, and grant my wish. I'll never ask for anything again. Please, God . . .*

There was a break in the wave of people. The silhouette of a man sat on the bottom step, leaning against the wall. He was missing an arm, and one of his legs didn't look like it would function; he had thrown that leg in front of him, and slumped over as if dead.

Kieli stopped a few steps above him.

His closed eyelashes twitched slightly, and Harvey opened his eyes. He raised his copper-colored head slowly, looked up at her, and smiled wryly, an exhausted look on his face. "I couldn't climb the stairs. Give me a hand," he said, as if nothing was wrong.

"You're late, darn it. I got tired of waiting . . ." Kieli murmured in a trembling voice, bending over and offering her hand. Harvey laboriously lifted his one remaining arm, took Kieli's hand, then closed his eyes and pressed the back of her hand to his forehead.

"Harvey?"

"It's nothing." He muttered something shortly under his breath. She got the feeling he had said, "Thank you."

In the distance, a bell started to ring, signaling the departure of the eastbound train.

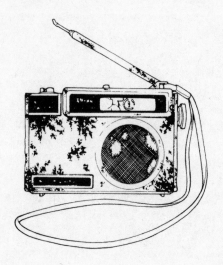

AFTERWORD

The complex I've lived in for five years is an iron-enforced five-story building three buildings away from the railroad, so even with my window closed, I constantly hear the muffled sounds of the railroad crossing alarm and the trains passing by. When I started living here, the noise drove me crazy, but now it's completely become a part of my life, and I let the sounds go by like background music. (But I can't get used to the dreadful singing that comes from the Japanese ballad karaoke at the snack bar diagonally across from me every night, as if it's cursing the world; I wish they would spare me that.)

Pleased to meet you. I'm Yukako Kabei.

This work received acclaim I couldn't have even hoped for in the form of the grand prize in the ninth Dengeki Game Novel Awards, and, maybe because I wrote it while listening to the sounds of the first morning train after staying up all night in an eight-tatami one-room apartment, it's a story with a decayed sort of tone, that mainly takes place on a train trip. It's also a story about a girl with a complicated personality and a man who hates doing anything, getting together and being separated, and about a man who's tired of living regaining purpose in life.

Wasted planets, steampunk, old-fashioned radios, rusty machines, old oil. It would make me as happy as I could be if all of you who like dilapidated things and react to that kind of vocabulary like this book. Of course, I would be so much more happy if all of you who aren't like that like it, too.

Now then, for this to become a book as it has, I really did receive a lot of assistance from many people. I would like to use this space to express my gratitude.

To everyone who supported me, from the time the work was selected to its completion as a book, starting with the honorable people on the selection committee who gave me this chance. I was honestly surprised to find out how many people worked directly and indirectly in order to make this one book, especially the following:

Taue-san, my contemporary, who drew such wonderful illustrations that the story can't hold a candle to them. (It's true. I'm in trouble.) When he showed me the roughs, I would always okay Kieli right away, but I would give him hard-to-understand requests about Harvey, like "He's too clean-cut; make him dirtier and more sloppy, slovenly, and scruffy," but he never complained and met my requests.

Everyone around me who supported me in my dangerous mental state while I was working on writing my submission, and Reiko-neesan from Mexico who always helps me out. I've really made you worry, but since I've started being able to write novels as a legitimate form of work, I've started legitimately neglecting my health, and I'm the same failure at life as always. I'm sorry, I'm sorry, I'll be careful.

The people at the coffee shop three stations away where I do most of my writing. I've troubled you unreasonably by coming in every weekend and sitting there with my laptop for five, six hours. I still do.

And finally, of course, to you, who are holding this book, I give you my highest thanks. I hope I get a chance to see you again.

Yukako Kabei

story by YUKAKO KABEI
art by SHIORI TESHIROGI

CHECK OUT A PREVIEW OF THE MANGA ADAPTATION OF KIELI

Please flip your book over to the "back" to enjoy a preview of the manga version of *KIELI* currently in stores!

If you're not already familiar with manga, it's worth pointing out that Japanese reads right to left so you should move through the panels and pages in "reverse" order.

KIELI PREVIEW

**YUKAKO KABEI
SHIORI TESHIROGI**

Translation: Alethea Nibley and Athena Nibley

Lettering: Alexis Eckerman

KIELI: SHISHATACHI WA KOYA NI NEMURU, Vol. 1
© 2006 YUKAKO KABEI
© 2006 SHIORI TESHIROGI
Licensed by KADOKAWA CORPORATION   ASCII MEDIA WORKS
All rights reserved. First published in Japan in 2006 by Akita Publishing Co., Ltd., Tokyo. English translation rights arranged with Akita Publishing Co., Ltd. through Tuttle-Mori Agency, Inc., Tokyo.

Translation © 2008 by Hachette Book Group, Inc.

Yen Press
Hachette Book Group
1290 Avenue of the Americas, New York, NY 10104

www.HachetteBookGroup.com
www.YenPress.com

Yen Press is an imprint of Hachette Book Group, Inc. The Yen Press name and logo are trademarks of Hachette Book Group, Inc.

Printed in the United States of America

ON THIS PLANET...

...THERE IS NO GOD.

GARAAAN (CLANG)

GARAAAN

LONG, LONG AGO...

...THE SAINTS ARRIVED ON THIS PLANET AFTER TRAVERSING SPACE FOR HUNDREDS OF YEARS AND FOUNDED A CHURCH. THAT'S WHAT THE DISTINGUISHED MEMBERS OF SOCIETY SAY.

HEY, GRANDMA!

AFTER TODAY'S SERVICE, I FINALLY GET IT!

GARAAAN

GARAAAN

BAN
(BANG)

GASHA
(KACHAK)

THE PLANET'S RESOURCES WERE DEPLETED, BRINGING THE WAR TO A CLOSE. AFTER THE WAR, THE CHURCH CARRIED OUT A LARGE-SCALE UNDYING HUNT.

SHIIII-IIIIIIIII-IIIIIIT!!

IT IS SAID THAT THE UNDYING WENT FROM BEING HUNTERS TO THE HUNTED, AND WERE EXTERMINATED, LEAVING ONLY THEIR LEGEND BEHIND.

DEMONS OF WAR. MEN WHO WENT AGAINST GOD'S WILL.

THEN EIGHTY YEARS PASSED.

CHAPTER 1
ROOMMATE

ONCE, THIS PLANET HAD A LARGE-SCALE WAR OVER ITS ABUNDANT RESOURCES.

IN THE FINAL STAGES OF THE WAR, THROUGH THE CRYSTALLIZATION OF TECHNOLOGY AND ULTRA-PURE ENERGY...

...A NEW KIND OF HUMAN WEAPON WAS BORN FROM THE RECYCLED BODIES OF FALLEN SOLDIERS. THEY WERE KNOWN AS...

...THE UNDYING.